OLYMPIAN NIGHTS

John Kendrick Bangs

1st WORLD
LIBRARY
Literary Society

Olympian Nights

John Kendrick Bangs

© 1st World Library – Literary Society, 2005
PO Box 2211
Fairfield, IA 52556
www.1stworldlibrary.org
First Edition

LCCN: 2006902738

Softcover ISBN: 1-4218-1868-X
Hardcover ISBN: 1-4218-1768-3
eBook ISBN: 1-4218-1968-6

Purchase *"Olympian Nights"*
as a traditional bound book at:
www.1stWorldLibrary.org/purchase.asp?ISBN=1-4218-1868-X

1st World Library Literary Society is a nonprofit
organization dedicated to promoting literacy by:

- Creating a free internet library accessible from any computer worldwide.
- Hosting writing competitions and offering book publishing scholarships.

Olympian Nights
contributed by Tim, Ed & Rodney
in support of
1st World Library Literary Society

CONTENTS

I

I REACH MOUNT OLYMPUS

While travelling through the classic realms of Greece some years ago, sincerely desirous of discovering the lurking-place of a certain war which the newspapers of my own country were describing with some vividness, I chanced upon the base of the far-famed Mount Olympus. Night was coming on apace and I was tired, having been led during the day upon a wild-goose chase by my guide, who had assured me that he had definitely located the scene of hostilities between the Greeks and the Turks. He had promised that for a consideration I should witness a conflict between the contending armies which in its sanguinary aspects should surpass anything the world had yet known. Whether or not it so happened that the armies had been booked for a public exhibition elsewhere, unknown to the talented bandit who was acting as my courier, I am not aware, but, as the event transpired, the search was futile, and another day was wasted. Most annoying, too, was the fact that I dared not manifest the impatience which I naturally felt. I am not remarkable as a specimen of the strong man; quite the reverse indeed, for, while I am by no means a weakling, I am no adept in the fistic art. Hence, when my guide, Hippopopolis by name, as the sun sank behind the western hills, informed me that I was again to be disappointed, the fact that he stands six feet two in his stockings, when he wears them, and has a pleasing way of bending crowbars as a pastime, led me to conceal the irritation which I felt.

"It's all right, Hippopopolis," I said, swallowing my wrath. "It's all right. We've had a good bit of exercise, anyhow, and that, after all, is the chief desideratum to a man of a sedentary occupation. How many miles have we walked?"

"Oh, about forty-three," he said, calmly. "A short distance, your Excellency."

"Very - very short," said I, rubbing my aching calves. "In my own country I make a practice of walking at least a hundred every day. It's quite a pleasing stroll from my home in New York over to Philadelphia and back. I hope I shall be able to show it you some day."

"It will be altogether charming, Excellency," said he. "Shall we - ah - walk back to Athens now, or would you prefer to rest here for the night?"

"I - I guess I'll stay here, Hippopopolis," I replied. "This seems to be a very comfortable sort of a mountain in front of us, and the air is soft. Suppose we rest in the soothing shade for the night? It would be quite an adventure."

"As your Excellency wishes," he replied, tossing a bowlder into the air and catching it with ease as it came down. "It is not often done, but it is for you to say."

"What mountain is it, Hippopopolis?" I asked, turning and gazing at the eminence before us.

"It is Mount Olympus," he answered.

"What?" I cried. "Not the home of the gods?"

"The very same, your Excellency," he acquiesced. "At least, that is the report. It is commonly stated hereabouts that the god-trust has its headquarters here. As for myself, I have explored its every nook and cranny, but I never saw any gods on it. It's my private opinion that they've moved away; though

John Kendrick Bangs

there be those who claim that it is still occupied by the former rulers of destiny living incog. Like other well-born rogues who desire to avoid notoriety."

Hippopopolis is a decided democrat in his views, and has less respect for the King than he has for the peasant.

"I shouldn't call them rogues exactly," I ventured. "Some of 'em were a pretty respectable lot. There was Apollo and old Jupiter himself, and -"

"Oh, you can't tell me anything about them," retorted Hippopopolis. "I haven't been born and bred in this country for nothing, your Excellency. They were a bad lot all through. Shall I prepare your supper?"

"If you please, Hippopopolis," said I, throwing myself down beneath a huge tree and giving myself up to the reveries of the moment. I did not deem it well to interpose too strongly between Hippopopolis and his views of the immortals just then. He had always a glitter in his eye when any one ventured to controvert his assertions which made a debate with him a thing to be apprehended. Still, I did not exactly like to yield, for, to tell the truth, the Olympian folk have always interested me hugely, and, while I would not of course endorse any one of them for a high public trust in these days, I have admired them for their many remarkable qualities.

"Of course," said I, reverting to the question a few moments later, as Hippopopolis opened a box of sardines and set the bread a-toasting on the fire he had made. "Of course, I should not venture to say that I, a stranger, know as much about the private habits of the gods as do you, who have been their neighbor; but that they are rogues is news to me."

"That may be, too," said Hippopopolis. "People are often thought more of by strangers than by their own fellow-townsmen. Even you, sir, I might suspect, who are by these simple Greeks supposed to be a sort of reigning sovereign in your own country, are not at home, perhaps, so large a hill of potatoes. So with Jupiter and Apollo and Mercury, and the ladies of the court. I haven't a doubt that in the United States you think Jupiter a remarkably great man, and Apollo a musician, and Mercury a gentleman of some business capacity, but we Greeks know better. And as for the ladies - hum - well, your Excellency, they are not received. They are too bold and pushing. They lack the refinements, and as for their beauty and accomplishments -"

Hippopopolis here indulged in a gesture which betokened excessive scorn of the beauty and accomplishments of the ladies of Olympus.

"You have never seen these people, Hippopopolis?" I asked.

"I have been spared that necessity," said he, "but I know all about them, and I assert to you upon my honor as a courier and the best guide in the Archipelago that Jupiter is the worst old *roue* a country ever had saddled upon it; Apollo's music would drive you mad and make you welcome a xylophone duet; and as for Mercury's business capacity, that is merely a capacity for getting away from his creditors. Why shouldn't a man wax rich if, after floating a thousand bogus corporations, selling the stock at par and putting the money into his own pocket, he could unfold his wings and fly off into the empyrean, leaving his stock and bond holders to mourn their loss?"

"Excuse me, Hippopopolis," I put in, interrupting him fearlessly for the moment, "pray don't try to deceive me by any such statement as that. I don't know very much, but I know something about Mercury, and when you say he puts other people's money into his pockets, I am in a position to prove otherwise. From five years of age up to the present time I have been brought up in a home where a bronze statue of Mercury, said to be the most perfect resemblance in all the statuary of the world, classic or otherwise, has been the most conspicuous ornament. At ten I could reproduce on paper with my pencil every line, every shade, every curve, every movement of the effigy in so far as my artistic talent would permit, and I know that Mercury not only had no pocket, but wore no garments in which even so little as a change pocket could have been concealed. Wherefore there must be some mistake about your charge."

Hippopopolis laughed.

"Humph!" he said. "It is very evident that you people over the sea have very superficial notions of things here. When Mercury posed for that statue, like most of you people who have your photographs taken, he posed in full evening dress. That is why there is so little of it in evidence. But in his business suit, Mercury is a very different sort of a person. Even in Olympus he'd have been ruled off the stock exchange if he'd ventured to appear there as scantily attired as he is in most of his statuary appearances. You certainly are not so green as to suppose that that suit he wears in his statues is the whole extent of his wardrobe?"

"I had supposed so," I confessed. "It's a trifle unconventional; but, then, he's one of the gods, and, I presumed, could dress as he pleased. Your gods are independent, I should imagine, of the mere decrees of fashion."

"The more exalted one's position, the greater the sartorial obligation," retorted Hippopopolis, who, for a Greek and a guide, had, as will be seen, a vocabulary of most remarkable range. "Just as it happens that our King here, like H. R. H. the Prince of Wales, has to be provided with seven hundred and sixty-eight suits of clothes so as to be properly clad at the variety of functions he is required to grace, so does a god have to be provided with a wardrobe of rare quality and extent. For drawing-room tables, mantel-pieces, and pedestals, otherwise for statuary, Mercury can go about clad in just about half as much stuff as it would require to cover a fairly sized sofa-cushion and not arouse drastic criticism; but when he goes to business he is as well provided with pockets as any other speculator."

"Another idol shattered!" I cried, in mock grief. "But Apollo, Hippopopolis - Apollo! Do not tell me he is not a virtuoso of rare technique on the lyre!"

"His technique is more than rare," sneered Hippopopolis. "It is excessively raw. It has been said by men who have heard both that Nero of Hades can do more to move an audience with his fiddle with two strings broken and his bow wrist sprained than Apollo can do with the aid of his lyre and a special dispensation of divine inspiration from Zeus himself."

"There are various ways of moving audiences, Hippopopolis," I ventured. "Now Nero, I should say, could move an audience - out of the hall - in a very few moments. In fact, I have always believed that that is why he fiddled when Rome was burning: so that people would run out of the city limits before they perished."

"It's a very droll view," laughed Hippopopolis, "and I dare say holds much of the truth; but Nero's faulty execution is not proof of Apollo's virtuosity. For a woodland musicale given by the Dryads, say, to their friends, the squirrels and moles and wild-cats, and other denizens of the forest, Apollo will suffice. The musical taste of a kangaroo might find the strumming of his lyre by Apollo to its liking, but for cultivated people who know a crescendo andante-arpeggio from the staccato tones of a penny whistle, he is inadequate."

"You speak as if you had heard the god," said I.

"I have not," retorted Hippopopolis, "but I have heard playing by people, generally beginners, of whom the rural press has said that he - or more often she - has the touch of an Apollo, and, if that is true, as are all things we read in the newspapers, particularly the rural papers, which are not so sophisticated as to lie, then Apollo would better not attempt to play at one of our Athenian Courier Association Smokers. I venture to assert that if he did he would have to be carried home with a bandage about his brow instead of a laurel, and his cherished lyre would become but a memory."

I turned sadly to my supper. I had found the mundane things of Greece disappointing enough, but my sorrow over Hippopopolis's expert testimony as to the shortcoming of the gods was overwhelming. It was to be expected that the country would fall into a decadent state sooner or later, but that the Olympians themselves were not all that they were cracked up to be by the mythologies had never suggested itself to me. As a result of my courier's words, I lapsed into a moody silence, which by eight o'clock developed into an irresistible desire to sleep.

"I'll take a nap, Hippopopolis," said I, rolling my coat into a bundle and placing it under my head. "You will, I trust, be good enough to stand guard lest some of these gods you have mentioned come and pick my pockets?" I added, satirically.

"I will see that the gods do not rob you," he returned, dryly, with a slight emphasis on the word "gods," the significance of which I did not at the moment take in, but which later developments made all too clear.

Three minutes later I slept soundly.

At ten o'clock, about, I awoke with a start. The fire was out and I was alone. Hippopopolis had disappeared and with him had gone my watch, the contents of my pocket-book, my letter of credit, and everything of value I had with me, with the exception of my shirt-studs, which, I presume, would have gone also had they not been fastened to me in such a way that, in getting them, Hippopopolis would have had to wake me up.

To add to my plight, the rain was pouring down in torrents.

II

I SEEK SHELTER AND FIND IT

"This is a fine piece of business," I said to myself, springing to my feet. And then I called as loudly as my lungs would permit for Hippopopolis. It was really exhilarating to do so. The name lends itself so readily to a sonorous effect. The hills fairly echoed and re-echoed with the name, but no answer came, and finally I gave up in disgust, seeking meanwhile the very inadequate shelter of a tree, to keep the rain off. A more woebegone picture never presented itself, I am convinced. I was chilled through, shivering in the dampness of the night, a steady stream of water pouring upon and drenching my clothing, void of property of an available nature, and lost in a strange land. To make matters worse, I was familiar only with classic Greek, which language is utterly unknown in those parts to-day, being spoken only by the professors of the American school at Athens and the war correspondents of the New York Sunday newspapers - a fact, by the way, which probably accounts for the latter's unfamiliarity with classic English. It is too much in these times to expect a man to speak or write more than one language at a time. Even if I survived the exposure of the night, a horrid death by starvation stared me in the face, since I had no means of conveying to any one who might appear the idea that I was hungry.

Still, if starvation was to be my lot, I preferred to starve dryly and warmly; so, deserting the tree which was now rather worse as a refuge than no refuge at all, since the limbs began to trickle forth steady streams of water, which, by some accursed miracle of choice, seemed to consider the back of my neck their inevitable destination, I started in to explore as best I could in the uncanny light of the night for some more sheltered nook. Feeling, too, that, having robbed me, Hippopopolis would become an extremely unpleasant person to encounter in my unarmed and exhausted state, I made my way up the mountainside, rather than down into the valley, where my inconsiderate guide was probably even then engaged in squandering my hard-earned wealth, in company with the peasants of that locality, who see real money so seldom that they ask no unpleasant questions as to whence it has come when they do see it.

"Under the circumstances," thought I, "I sincerely hope that the paths of Hippopopolis and myself may lie as wide as the poles apart. If so be we do again tread the same path, I trust I shall see him in time to be able to ignore his presence."

With this reflection I made my way with difficulty up the side of Olympus. Several times it seemed to me that I had found the spot wherein I might lie until the sun should rise, but quite as often an inconsiderate leak overhead through the leaves of the trees, or an undiscovered crack in the rocks above me, sent me travelling upon my way. Physical endurance has its limits, however, and at the end of a two hours' climb, wellnigh exhausted, I staggered into an opening between two walls of rock, and fell almost fainting to the ground. The falling rain revived me, and on my hands and knees I crawled farther in, and, to my great delight, shortly found myself in a high-ceiled cavern, safe from the storm, a place in which one might starve comfortably, if so be one had to pass through that trying ordeal.

"He might have left me my flask," I groaned as I thought over the pint of warming liquid which Hippopopolis had taken from me. It was of a particular sort, and I liked it whether I was thirsty or not. "If he'd only left me that, he might have had my letter of credit, and no questions asked. These Greeks are apparently not aware that there is consideration even among thieves."

Huddling myself together, I tried to get warm after the fashion of the small boy when he jumps into his cold-sheeted bed on a winter's night, a process which makes his legs warm the upper part of his body, and *vice versa*. It was moderately successful. If I could have wrung the water out of my clothes, it might have been wholly so. Still, matters began to look more cheerful, and I was about to drop off into a doze, when at the far end of the cavern, where all had hitherto been black as night, there suddenly burst forth a tremendous flood of light.

"Humph!" thought I, as the rays pierced through the blackness of the cavern even to where I lay shivering. "I'm in for it now. In all probability I have stumbled upon a bandits' cave."

Pleasing visions of the ways of bandits began to flit through my mind.

"In all likelihood," thought I, "there are seventeen of them. As I have read my fiction, there are invariably seventeen bandits to a band. It's like sixteen ounces to the pound, or three feet to the yard, or fifty-three cents to the dollar. It never varies. What hope have I to escape unharmed from seventeen bandits, even though five of them are discontented - as is always the case in books - and are ready to betray their chief to the enemy? I am the enemy, of course, but I'll be hanged if I wish the chief betrayed into my hands. He could probably thrash me single-handed. My hands are full anyhow, whether I get the chief or not."

My heart sank into my boots; but as these were very wet, it promptly returned to my throat, where it had rested ever since Hippopopolis had deserted me. My heart is a very sane sort of an organ. I gazed towards the light intently, expecting to see dark figures of murderous mould loom up before me, but in this I was agreeably disappointed. Nothing of the sort happened, and I grew easier in my mind, although my curiosity was by no means appeased.

"I know what I will do," I said to myself. "I'll make friends with the chief himself. That's the best plan. If he is responsive, my family will be spared the necessity of receiving one of my ears by mail with a delicate request for $20,000 ransom, accompanied by a P. S. enclosing the other ear to emphasize the importance of the complication."

By way of diversion, let me say here that, while slicing off the victim's ear is a staple situation among novelists who write of bandits, in all my experience with bandits - and I have known a thousand, most of 'em in Wall Street - I have never known it done, and I challenge those who write of South European highway-robbers to produce any evidence to prove that the habit is prevalent. The idea is, on the face of it, invalid. The ears of mankind, despite certain differences which are acknowledged, are, after all, very much alike. The point that differentiates one ear from another is the angle at which it is set from the head. The angle, according to the most scientific students of the organ of hearing, is the basis of the estimate of the individual. Therefore, to convince the wealthy persons at home that large sums of money are expected of them to preserve the life of the father of the family, the truly expert bandit must send something besides the ear itself, which, when cut off, has no angle whatsoever. If I, who am no bandit, and who have not studied the art of the banditti, may make a suggestion which may prove valuable to the highwaymen of Italy and Greece, the only sure method of identifying the individual lies in the cutting off of the head of the victim, by which means alone the identity of the person to be ransomed may be settled beyond all question. As one who has suffered, I will say that I would not send a check for $20,000 to a bandit on the testimony of one ear any more than I would lend a man ten dollars on his own representation as to the meals he had not had, the drinks he wanted, or the date upon which he would pay it back.

All these ideas flashed across my mind as I lay there worn in spirit and chilled to the bone. At last, however, after a considerable effort, I gathered myself together and resolved to investigate. I rose up, stood uncertainly on my feet, and was about to make my way towards the sources of the unexpected light, when a dark figure rushed past me. I tried to speak to it.

"Hello, there!" said I, hoping to gain its attention and ask its advice, since it came into the cavern in that breezy fashion which betokens familiarity with surroundings. The being, whatever it really was, and I was soon to find this out, turned a scornful and really majestic face upon me, as much as to say, "Who are you that should thus address a god?" The rushing thing wore a crown and flowing robes. Likewise it had a gray beard and an air of power which made me, a mere mortal, seem weak even in my own estimation. Furthermore, there was a divine atmosphere following in his wake. It suggested the most brilliant of brilliantine.

"Here," he cried as he passed. "I haven't time to listen to your story, but here is my card. I have no change about me. Call upon me to-morrow and I will attend to your needs."

The card fluttered to my side, and, not being a mendicant, I paid little attention to it, preferring to watch this fast-disappearing figure until I should see whither it was going. Arriving at the far end of the cavern, the hurrying figure stopped and apparently pushed a button at the side of the wall. Immediately an iron door, which I had not before perceived, was pushed aside. The dark figure disappeared into what seemed to be a well-lighted elevator, and was promptly lifted out of sight. All became dark again, and I was frankly puzzled. This was a situation beyond my ken. What it could mean I could not surmise, and in the hope of finding a clew to the mystery I groped about in the darkness for the card which the hurried individual had cast at me with his words of encouragement. Ultimately I found it, but was unable to decipher its inscription, if perchance it had one. Nevertheless, I managed to keep my spirits up. This, I think, was a Herculean task, considering the darkness and my extreme lonesomeness. I can be happy under adverse circumstances, if only I have congenial company. But to lie alone, in a black cavern, prey only to the thoughts of my environment, thoughts suggesting all things apart from life, thoughts which send the mind over the past a thousand centuries removed - these are not comforting, and these were the only thoughts vouchsafed to me.

A half-hour was thus passed in the darkness, and then the light appeared again, and I resolved, though little strength was left to me, to seek out its source. I stood up and staggered towards it, and as I drew nearer observed that the illumination came from nothing more nor less than an elevator at the bottom of a shaft, the magnitude of which I could not, of course, at the moment determine.

The boy in charge was a pretty little chap, and, if I may so state it, was absolutely unclad, but about his shoulders was slung a strap which in turn held a leathern bag, which, to my eyes, suggested a golf-bag more than anything else, except that it was filled with arrows instead of golf-clubs.

"How do you do?" said I, politely. "Whose caddy are you?"

"Very well," said the little lad. "Not much to brag of, however. Merely bobbish, pretty bobbish. In answer to your second question, I take pleasure in informing you," he added, "that I am everybody's caddy."

"You are - the elevator boy?" I queried, with some hesitation.

"That is my present position," said he.

"And, ah, whither do you elevate, my lad?"

"Up!" said he, after the manner of one who does not wish to commit himself, like most elevator boys. "But whom do you wish to see?" he demanded, trying hard to frown and succeeding only in making a ludicrous exhibition of himself.

Frankly, I did not know, but under the impulse of the moment I handed out the card which the stranger had thrown to me.

"I forget the gentleman's name," said I, "but here is his card. He asked me to call."

The elevator boy glanced at it, and his manner immediately changed.

"Oh, indeed. Very well, sir," he said. "I'll take you up right away. Step lively, please."

I stepped into the elevator, and the lad turned a wheel which set us upon our upward journey at once.

"I am sorry to have been so rude to you, sir," said the boy. "I didn't really know you were a friend of his."

"Of whom?" I demanded.

"The old man himself," he replied, with which he handed me back the card I had given him, upon reading which I ascertained the name of the individual who had rushed past me so unceremoniously.

The card was this:

MR. JUPITER JOVE ZEUS

MOUNT OLYMPUS
GREECE

"Top floor, sir," said the elevator boy, obsequiously.

John Kendrick Bangs

III

THE ELEVATOR BOY

"Known the old man long, sir?" queried the boy as we ascended.

"By reputation," said I.

"Humph!" said the lad. "Can't have a very good opinion of him, then. It's a good thing you are going to have a little personal experience with him. He's not a bad lot, after all. Rotten things said of him, but then - you know, eh?"

"Oh, as for that," said I, "I don't think his reputation is so dreadful. To be sure, there have been one or two little indiscretions connected with his past, and at times he has seemed a bit vindictive in chucking thunder-bolts at his enemies, but, on the whole, I fancy he's behaved himself pretty well."

"True," said the boy. "And then you've got to take his bringing-up into consideration. Things which would be altogether wrong in the son of a Presbyterian clergyman would not be unbecoming in a descendant of old Father Time. Jupiter is, after all, a self-made immortal, and the fact that his parents, old Mr. and Mrs. Cronos, let him grow up sort of wild, naturally left its impress on his character."

"Of course," said I, somewhat amused to hear the Thunderer's character analyzed by a mere infant. "But how about yourself, my laddie? Are you anybody in particular? You look like a cherub."

"Some folks call me Dan," said the boy, "and I *am* somebody in particular. Fact is, sir, if it hadn't been for me there wouldn't have been anybody in particular anywhere. I'm Cupid, sir, God of Love, favorite son of Venus, at your service."

"And husband of the delectable Psyche?" I cried, recalling certain facts I had learned. "You look awfully young to be married."

"Hum - well, I was, and I am, but we've separated," the boy replied, with a note of sadness in his voice. "She was a very nice little person, that Psyche - one of the best ever, I assure you - but she was too much of a butterfly to be the perpetual confidante of a person charged with such important matters as I am. Besides, she didn't get on with mother."

"Seems to me that I have heard that Madame Venus did not approve of the match," I vouchsafed.

"No. She didn't from the start," said Cupid. "Psyche was too pretty, and ma rather wanted to corner all the feminine beauty in our family; but I had my way in the end. I generally do," the little chap added, with a chuckle.

"But the separation, my dear boy?" I put in. "I am awfully sorry to hear of that. I, in common with most mortals, supposed that the marriage was idyllic."

"It was," said Cupid, "and therefore not practical enough to be a good investment. You see, sir, there was a time when the love affairs of the universe were intrusted to my care. Lovers everywhere came to me to confide their woes, and I was doing a great business. Everybody was pleased with my way of conducting my department. I seemed to have a special genius for managing a love affair. Even persons who were opposed to the administration conceded that the Under Secretary of Home Affairs - myself - was assured of a cabinet office for life, whatever party was in power. If Pluto had been able to get elected, the force of public opinion would have kept me in office. Then I married, myself, and things changed. Like a dutiful husband, I had no secrets from my wife. I couldn't have had if I had wanted to. Psyche's curiosity was a close second to Pandora's, and, if she wanted to know anything, there was never any peace in the family until she found out all about it. Still, I didn't wish to have any secrets from her. As a scientific expert in Love, I knew that the surest basis of a lasting happiness lay in mutual confidence. Hence, I told Psyche all I knew, and it got her into trouble right away."

"She - ah - couldn't keep a secret?" I asked.

"At first she could," said Cupid. "That was the cause of the first row between her and Venus. Mother got mad as a hatter with her one morning after breakfast because Psyche *could* keep a secret. There was a little affair on between Jupiter and a certain person whose name I shall not mention, and I had charge of it. Of course, I told Psyche all about it, and in some way known only to woman she managed to convey to Venus the notion that she knew all about it, but couldn't tell, and, still further, wouldn't tell. I'd gone down-town to business, leaving everything peaceful and happy, but when I got back to luncheon - Great Chaos, it was awful! The two ladies were not on speaking terms, and I had to put on a fur overcoat to keep from freezing to death in the atmosphere that had arisen between them. It was six inches below zero - and the way those two would sniff and sneer at each other was a caution."

"I quite understand the situation," I said, sympathetically.

"No doubt," said Cupid. "You can also possibly understand how a quarrel between the only two women you ever loved could incapacitate you for your duties. For ten days after that I was simply incapable of directing the love affairs of the universe properly. Persons I'd designed for each other were given to others, and a great deal of unhappiness resulted. There were nine thousand six hundred and seventy-six divorces as the result of that week's work. It's a terrible situation for a well-meaning chap to have to decide between his wife and his mother."

"Never had it," said I; "but I can imagine it."

"Don't think you can," sighed Cupid. "There are situations in real life, sir, which surpass the wildest flights of the imagination. That is why truth is stranger than fiction. However," he added, his face brightening, "it was a useful experience to me in my professional work. I learned for the first time that when a mother-in-law comes in at the door, intending to remain indefinitely, love flies out at the window. Or, as Solomon - I believe it was Solomon. He wrote Proverbs, did he not?"

"Yes," said I. "He and Josh Billings."

"Well," vouchsafed Cupid, "I can't swear as to the authorship of the proverb, but some proverbialist said 'Two is company and three is a crowd.' I'd never known that before, but I learned it then, and began to stay away from home a little myself, so that we should not be crowded."

I commended the young man for his philosophy.

"Nevertheless, my dear Dan," I added, "you ought to be more autocratic. Knowing that two is company and three otherwise, you have been guilty of allowing many a young couple who have trusted in you to begin house-keeping with an inevitable third person. We see it every day among the mortals."

"What has been good enough for me, sir," the boy returned, with a comical assumption of sternness - he looked so like a fat baby of three just ready for his bath - "is good enough for mortals. When I married Psyche, I brought her home to my mother's house, and for some nineteen thousand years we lived together. If Love can stand it, mortals must."

"Excuse me," said I, apologetically. "I have not suffered. However, in all my study of you mythologians, it has never occurred to me before this that Venus was the goddess of the mother-in-law."

"You mustn't blame me for that," said Cupid, dryly. "I'm the god of Love; wisdom is out of my province. For what you don't know and haven't learned you must blame Pallas, who is our Superintendent of Public Instruction. She knows it all - and she got it darned easy, too. She sprang forth from the head of Jove with a Ph.D. already conferred upon her. She looks after the education of the world. I don't - but I'll wager you anything you please to put up that man gains more real experience under my management than he does from Athena's department, useful as her work is."

I could not but admit the truth of all that the boy said, and of course I told him so. To change the subject, which, if pursued, might lead to an exposure of my own ignorance, I said:

"But, Dan, what interests me most, and pains me most as well, is to hear that you are separated from Psyche. I do not wish to seem inquisitive on the subject of a - ah - of a man's family affairs" - I hesitated in my speech because he seemed such a baby and it was difficult to take him seriously, as is always the way with Love, unless we are directly involved - "but you have told me of the separation, and as a man, a newspaper-man, I am interested. Couldn't you reconcile your mother, Madame Venus, to Psyche - or, rather, Mrs. Dan?"

"Not for a moment," replied the boy. "Not for a millionth part of a tenth of a quarter of a second by a stop-watch. Their irreconcilability was copper-fastened, and I found myself compelled to choose between them. My mother developed a gray hair the day after the first trouble, and my wife began to go out to afternoon teas and sewing-circles and dances. The teas and dances were all right. You can't talk at either. But the sewing-circle was ruin. At this particular time the circle was engaged in making winter garments for the children of the mother of the Gracchi. I presume that as a student and as a father you realize all that this meant. You also know that a sewing-circle needs four things: first, an object; second, a needle and thread; third, a garment; fourth, a subject for conversation. These things are constitutionally required, and Psyche joined what she called 'The Immortal Dorcas.' The result was that all Olympus and half of Hades were shortly acquainted with the confidential workings of my department - all told under the inviolate bond of secrecy, however, which requires that each member confided in shall not communicate what she has heard to more - or to less - than ten people."

"I know," said I. "The Dorcas habit has followers among my own people."

"But see where it placed me!" cried the little creature. "There was me, or I - I don't know whether Greek or English is preferable to you - charged with the love affairs of the universe. Confiding all I knew, like a dutiful husband, to my wife, and having her letting it all out to the public through the society. Why, my dear fellow, it wasn't long before the immortals began to accuse me of being in the pay of the Sunday newspapers, and you must know as well as anybody else that Love has nothing to do with them. Even the affairs of my sovereign began to creep out, and innuendoes connecting Jupiter with people prominent in society were printed in the opposition organs."

"Poor chap!" said I, sympathetically. "I did not realize that you had to contend against the Sunday-newspaper nuisance as we mortals have."

"We have," he said, quickly, almost resignedly; "and they are ruining even Olympus itself. Still, I made a stand. Told Psyche she talked too much, and from that time on confided in her no more."

"And how did she take it?" I asked.

"She declined to take it at all," said Cupid, with a sigh. "She demanded that I should tell her everything on penalty of losing her - and I lost her. She left me a little over a thousand years ago, and my mother for the same reason sent me adrift fifteen hundred or more years ago. That is why I am eking out a living running an elevator," he added, sadly. "Still, I'm happy here. I go up when I feel sad, and go down when I feel glad. On the whole, I am as happy as any of the gods."

"However, Dan," I cried, sympathetically, slapping him on the back, "you have your official position, and that will keep you in - ah - well, you don't seem to need 'em, but it would keep you in clothes if you could be persuaded to wear them."

"No," said the little elevator boy, sadly. "I don't want 'em in this climate - nor are they necessary in any other. All over the world, my dear fellow, *true* love is ever warm."

There was a decided interval. I felt sorry for the little lad who had been a god and who had become an elevator boy, so I said to him:

"Never mind, Danny, you are sure of your office always."

"I wish it were so," said he, sadly. "But really, sir, it isn't. You may think that love rules all things nowadays, but that is a fallacy. Of late years a rival concern has sprung up. I have found my office subjected to a most annoying competition which has attracted away from me a large number of my closest followers. In the days when we acknowledged ourselves to be purely heathen, love was regarded with respect, but now all that is changed. Opposite my office in the government building there is a matrimonial corporation doing a very large business, by which the fees of my position are greatly reduced. Possibly after you have had your audience with Jove to-morrow you will take a turn about the city, in which event you will see this trust's big brazen sign. You can't miss it if you walk along Mercury Avenue. It reads:

MAMMON & CO.
Matchmakers

FORTUNES GUARANTEED:
HAPPINESS EXTRA

GEO. W. MAMMON
President

HORACE GREED
Gen'l Manager

BRANCH OFFICE
67 Gehenna Ave., Hades

"Dear me!" I cried. "Poor Love!"

"I don't need your sympathy," said the boy, quickly, drawing himself up proudly. "It can't last, this competition. Man and god kind will soon see the difference in the permanence of our respective output. This is only a temporary success they are having, and it often happens that the spurious articles put forth by Mammon & Company are brought over to me to be repaired. My sun will dawn again. You can't put out the fires in my furnaces as long as men and women are made from the old receipt."

Here the elevator stopped, and a rather attractive young woman appeared at the door.

"Here is where you get out, sir," said the elevator boy.

"You are Mr. -" began the girl.

"I am," I replied.

"I have orders to show you to number 609," she said. "The proprietor will see you to-morrow at eleven."

"Thank you very much," I replied, somewhat overcome by the cordiality of my reception. It is not often that mere beggars are so hospitably received.

"Good-night, Cupid," I added, turning to the little chap in the elevator. "I trust we shall meet again."

"Oh, I guess we will," he replied, with a wink at the maid. "I generally do meet most men two or three times in their lives. So *au revoir* to you. Treat the gentleman well, Hebe," he concluded, pulling the rope to send the elevator back. "He doesn't know much, but he is sympathetic."

"I will, Danny, for your sake," said the little maid, archly.

The boy laughed and the car faded from sight. Hebe, even more lovely than has been claimed, with a charmingly demure glance at my costume, which was wofully bedraggled and wet, said:

"This way, sir. I will have your luggage sent to your room at once."

"But I haven't any luggage, my dear," said I. "I have only what is on my back."

"Ah, but you have," she replied, sweetly. "The proprietor has attended to that. There are five trunks, a hat-box, and a Gladstone bag already on their way up."

And with this she showed me into a magnificent apartment, and, even as she had said, within five minutes my luggage arrived, a valet appeared, unpacked the trunks and bag, brushed off the hat that had lain in the hat-box, and vanished, leaving me to my own reflections.

Surely Olympus was a great place, where one who appeared in the guise of a beggar was treated like a regiment of prodigal sons, furnished with a gorgeous apartment, and supplied with a wardrobe that would have aroused the envy of a reigning sovereign.

IV

I SUMMON A VALET

The room to which I was assigned was regal in its magnificence, and yet comfortable. Few modern hotels afforded anything like it, and, tired as I was, I could not venture to rest until I had investigated it and its contents thoroughly. It was, I should say, about twenty by thirty feet in its dimensions, and lighted by a soft, mellow glow that sprang forth from all parts without any visible source of supply. At the far end was a huge window, before which were drawn portieres of rich material in most graceful folds. Pulling these to one side, so that I might see what the outlook from the window might be, I staggered back appalled at the infinite grandeur of what lay before my eyes. It seemed as if all space were there, and yet within the compass of my vision. Planets which to my eye had hitherto been but twinkling specks of light in the blackness of the heavens became peopled worlds, which I could see in detail and recognize. Mars with its canals, Saturn with its rings - all were there before me, seemingly within reach of my outstretched hand. The world in which I lived appeared to have been removed from the middle distance, and those things which had rested beyond the ken of the mortal mind brought to my very feet, to be seen and touched and comprehended.

Then I threw the window open, and all was changed. The distant objects faded, and a beautiful golden city greeted my eyes - the city of Olympus, in which I was to pass so many happy hours. For the instant I was puzzled. Why at one moment the treasures of the universe of space had greeted my vision, and how all that had faded and the immediate surroundings of a celestial city lay before me, were not easy to understand. I drew back and closed the window again, and at once all became clear; the window-glass held the magic properties of the magnifying-lens, developed to an intensity which annihilated all space, and I began to see that the development of mortals in scientific matters was puny beside that of the gods in whose hands lay all the secrets of the universe, although the principles involved were in our full possession.

The situation overwhelmed me somewhat, and I drew the portieres together again. The feelings that came over me were similar to those that come to one standing on the edge of a great precipice gazing downward into the vast, black depths yawning at his feet. The giddiness that once, many years before, came upon me as I stood on the brink of the Niagaran cataract, which seemed irresistibly impelling me to join the mad rush of the waters, surged over me again, and I forced myself backward into the room, shutting out the sight, lest I should cast myself forth into the infinite space beyond. I threw myself down upon a couch and covered my eyes with my hands and tried to realize the situation. I was drunk with awe at all that was about me, and should, I think, have gone mad trying to comprehend its grandeur, had not my spirit been soothed by soft strains of music that now fell upon my ears.

I opened my eyes to discover whence the sounds had come, and even as the light streamed from unknown and unseen sources, so it was with the harmonies which followed, harmonies surpassing in beauty and swelling glory anything I had ever heard before.

And to these magnificent but soft and soothing strains I yielded myself up and slept. How long my sleep continued I have no means of knowing. It seemed to last but an instant, but when I opened my eyes once more I felt absolutely renewed in body and in spirit. The damp garments which I

John Kendrick Bangs

had worn when I fell back upon the couch had in some wise been removed, and when I stood up to indulge in the usual stretching of my limbs I found myself clad in an immaculate flowing robe of white, soft of texture, fastened at the neck with a jewelled brooch, and at the waist its fulness restrained by a girdle of gold. Furthermore, I had apparently been put through a process of ablution which left me with the cockles of my heart as warm as toast, and my whole being permeated with a glow of health which I had not known for many years. The aches in my bones, which I had feared on waking to find intensified, were gone; and if I could have retained permanently the aspect of vigor and beauty which was returned to me by the mirror when I stood before it, I should be in imminent danger of becoming conceited.

"I wonder," said I, as I gazed at myself in the mirror, "if this is the correct costume for breakfast. It's a slight drawback to know nothing of the customs of the locality in which you find yourself. Possibly an investigation of my new wardrobe will help me to decide."

I looked over the rich garments which had been provided, and found nothing which, according to my simple bringing up, suggested the idea that it was a good thing to wear at the morning meal.

"They ought to send me a valet," I murmured. "Perhaps they will if I ring for one. Where the deuce is the bell, I wonder?"

A search of the room soon divulged the resting-place of this desirable adjunct to the tourist's comfort. The dial system which has proved so successful in American hotels was in vogue here, except that it manifested a willingness on the part of the proprietor to provide the guest with a range of articles utterly beyond anything to be found in the purely mundane caravansary. I found that anything under the canopy that the mind of man could conceive of could be had by the mere pushing of a button. The disk of the electrical apparatus was divided off into many sections, calling respectively for saddle-horses, symphony concerts, ocean steamships, bath-towels, stenographers; cocktails of all sorts, and some sorts of which I had never before heard, and all of which I resolved to try in discreet sequence; manicures, chiropodists, astrologers, prophets, clergymen of all denominations, plots for novelists - indeed, anything that any person in any station of life might chance to desire could be got for the ringing.

My immediate need, however, was for a valet. Puzzled as to the manners and customs of the gods, I did not wish to make a bad appearance in the dining-room in a costume which should not be appropriate. I did think of ordering breakfast served in my room, but that seemed a very mortal and not a particularly godlike thing to do. Hence, I rang for a valet.

"I will tell him to get out my morning-suit, and no doubt he will select the thing I ought to wear," I said as I pressed the button.

The response was instant. My fingers had hardly left the button when a superb creature stood before me. Whence he sprang I do not know. There were no opening of doors, no traps or false panels, that I could see. The individual simply materialized.

"At your service, sir," said he, with a graceful obeisance.

"Pardon me," I replied, overcome once more by what was going on. "I - ah - think there must be some mistake. I - ah - I didn't ring for a god, I rang for a valet."

"I am the valet of Olympus, sir," he replied, gracefully flicking a speck of dust from the calf of his leg, the contour of which was beautiful to look upon, clad in superbly fitting silken tights. "Adonis, at your service. What can I do for you?"

"Well, I declare!" I cried, lost now in admiration of the way the gods were ordering things on Olympus. "So they've made you a valet, have they?"

"Yes," replied Adonis. "I hold office for the six months that I am here. You know that I am a resident of Olympus only half the time. The balance I live in Hades."

"It's a common custom," said I. "Even with us, our swellest people go south for the winter."

"Hum - yes," said Adonis, somewhat confused. "It's very good of you to draw that parallel. Your construction of the situation does credit to your sense of what is polite, sir. Unfortunately for me, however, my position is more like that of the habitual criminal who is sent to the penitentiary periodically. I have to go, whether I want to or not."

"Still, it must be a pleasant variation," I observed, forgetting that it is bad form to converse with a servant, and remembering only that I was addressing an old flame of Madame Venus. "Hades isn't a bad place for a little while, I should fancy."

"True," sighed Adonis. "But the society there is very mixed. It's full of self-made immortals, whereas we are all immortals by birth."

"And who, pray," I queried, "takes your place while you are below?"

"Narcissus," he replied; "but there's generally a lot of complaint about him. He takes more pains dressing himself than he does in looking after guests, the result of which is that after my departure things get topsy-turvy, and by the time I get back, with the exception of Narcissus, there isn't a well-dressed god in all Olympus."

"I wonder, where such perfection is possible," said I, "that they tolerate that."

"They're not going to very much longer," said Adonis, and then he laughed. "Narcissus queered himself last season at the palace. Jove sent for him to trim his beard, and he nearly cut one of the old man's ears off. Investigation showed that instead of keeping his eye on what he was doing, he was looking at himself in the glass all the time. Jupiter in his anger hurled a thunderbolt at him, but, fortunately for Narcissus, he hurled it at the mirrored and not at the real Narcissus, and he escaped. The result is the rumor that he will be made head-waiter in the dining-room instead of valet next season, in which event I shall probably be allowed to remain here all through the year, or else they'll put Jason on."

"And which would you prefer?" I asked.

"I think I'd rather have Jason put on," said Adonis. "While I don't care much for the climate of Hades, I am received there with much consideration socially, whereas up here I am only the valet. One doesn't mind being a nabob once in a while, you know. Besides - ah - don't say anything about it to anybody up here, but I'm getting a trifle tired of Venus. She is still beautiful, but you can't get over the idea that she's over four thousand years old. Furthermore, I met a little Fury down below last season who is simply ravishing." Here Adonis gave me a wink which made me rather curious to see the little Fury.

"Ah, Adonis, Adonis!" I cried, shaking my finger at him; "still up to your old tricks, are you?"

"Why not?" he demanded. "My character is formed. *Noblesse oblige* is a good motto for us all, only when one is born with *faiblesse* instead of *noblesse*, it becomes *faiblesse oblige*. Furthermore, sir, if I am to have the reputation, I must insist upon the perquisites."

What I replied to this bit of moralizing I shall not put down here, since I have no wish to commit myself thus publicly. I will say, however, that I did not blame the youthful-looking person unreservedly.

"Moreover, I have very fine apartments in Hades," he added,

"and I should hate to give them up. I live at the select home for gods and gentlemen, kept by Madame Persephone. When she takes an interest in one of her boarders she is a mighty fine landlady, and, like most ladies, if I may say it with all due modesty, she has taken an interest in me. The result is that I have the best suite in the house, overlooking the Styx, and as fine a table as any one could want. But I must ask your pardon, sir, for taking up so much of your time with my personal affairs. We both seem to have forgotten that I am here to wait upon you."

"It has been very interesting, Adonis," I said. "And if it's anybody's fault, it is mine. What I wished of you was that you should get out my breakfast-suit, so that I might dress and go to the dining-room."

"Certainly, sir," he replied, walking to the clothes-closet. "Pardon me, but - ah - what is your profession when at home?"

"Why do you ask?" I queried. "Not that I am unwilling to tell you, but -"

"I merely wished to guide my selection of your garments. If you are a naval officer, I will put out your admiral's uniform. If you are a professional golfer, I'll get out your red coat."

"I am a literary man," I said.

"Ah!" he observed, lifting his eyebrows. "Then, of course, you won't mind wearing these."

And he hauled forth a pair of black-and-white trousers with checks as large as the squares of a chessboard, a blue cloth vest with white polka dots, and a long, gray Prince Albert coat, with mauve satin lapels. The shirt was pink and blue, stripes of each alternating, running cross-ways, a white collar, and a flaring red four-in-hand tie!

"Great Scott, Adonis!" I cried. "Must I wear those?"

"You're under no compulsion to do so," said he. "But I thought you said you were a literary man."

"Well?"

"Well - literary men never care what they wear so long as they attract attention, do they?"

I laughed. "We are not all built that way, Adonis," said I. "Some of us are modest and have a little taste."

"Well, it's news to me," said he. "I guess it must be among the minor lights."

"It is - generally," said I. "And if you don't mind, I'd rather wear the golf clothes."

And I did.

V

THE OLYMPIAN LINKS

"There," said Adonis, as he put the finishing touch to my costume. "You look like a champion. Do you play golf, sir?"

"There's a difference of opinion about that, Adonis," I replied, my mind reverting to the number of handicap matches I hadn't won. "Some people who have observed my game say I don't. Have you links here?"

"Have we links?" he cried. "Well, rather. They're said to be the best in the universe."

"And are they handy?"

"Very - in the season."

"I don't quite catch the idea," I said.

"Oh, sometimes the course is nearer than it is at others. Come here a minute," he said, "and I'll point it out to you."

He drew me to the wonderful window of which I have already spoken, and through the powerful glass pointed in the direction of Mars.

"See that?" he said.

"Yes," I replied. "That is Mars."

"Exactly," said Adonis. "Mars is the Olympian links. His distance from here varies, as you are probably aware. When Mars is near aphelion he is 61,800,000 miles away, but in his perihelion he gets it down to 33,800,000. That's why we have our golf season while Mars is in his perihelion. It saves us 28,000,000 miles in getting there."

I laughed. "You call that handy, do you?" I said.

"Why not?" he asked. "It's a matter of five minutes on a bike, ten minutes in the automobile, and twenty minutes if you walk."

"Of course, Adonis," said I, "I'm not so green as to swallow all that. How the dickens can you walk through space?"

"You're vastly greener than you think you are," he retorted, rather uncivilly, perhaps, for a valet, but I paid no attention to that, preferring to take him, despite his menial capacity, in his godlike personality. "I might even say, sir, that your greenness is spacious. You judge us from your own mean, limited, mundane point of view. But you needn't think because you earth people cannot walk on air we Olympians are equally incapacitated. You can walk there in two ways. One of these is to fasten a pair of ankle-wings on your legs; the other is to purchase a pair of sky-scrapers. These are simple, consisting merely of boots with gas soles. You inflate the soles with gas and walk along. It's simple and easy, doesn't require any practice, and as long as you keep up in the air and don't step on church steeples or weather-vanes it's perfectly safe. Of course, if you stepped on a sharp-pointed weather-vane, or a lightning-rod, and punctured your sole, there's no telling what would happen."

"And how about the wings?" I asked.

"They're much more exhilarating, but a little dangerous if you don't know how to use them," Adonis replied. "Flying isn't any easier than roller-skating, and if you upset and get your head below your feet it's extremely difficult to right yourself again. If you try to go out there with ankle-wings, take my advice and wear a pair of small balloons about your chest to hold you right-end upward."

"I'll remember," said I, somewhat awed at the prospect of trying to walk through space with the aid of ankle-wings. "And how about the bicycle?" I added.

"If you can ride a bicycle on an ordinary road you'll have no trouble," he replied. "Keep your tires well filled with gas and avoid headers. If I were you, though, at first I'd go out on the automobile. It makes six round trips a day and it's absolutely safe. Being so high up in the air might make you dizzy, and you might find the bicycling too much for your nerves. After a little while you'll get used to enormous heights, and then, of course, you can go any old way you choose. The fare for the round trip is only fifteen hundred dollars."

"The automobile is in competent hands, eh?"

"Yes," said Adonis. "Phaeton has charge of it."

"Humph!" I sneered. "He's your idea of a competent driver, eh? He hasn't that reputation on earth. Was it an untruth that credits him with a fine smash-up when he tried to drive the chariot of the sun?"

"Not a bit of it," said Adonis. "That's all of it simple truth. I happen to know, because I saw the finish of the whole thing myself, and was one of the fellows who turned a fire-extinguisher on him and saved him from being a total loss to the insurance companies. But he learned his lesson. There's nothing like experience to teach caution, and that little episode gave Phaeton caution to burn, if I may indulge in mundane slang. He was guyed so unmercifully by everybody for his carelessness that the first thing he did when he recovered was to learn how to drive, and it wasn't six cycles before he was the most expert whip in Olympus. He finally made a profession of it and established a livery-stable. Then, when the automobile came in and horses went out of fashion, he kept up with the times, and is to-day in charge of all our rapid transit - he owns the franchises for the Jupiter and Dipper Trolley Road, he is the largest stockholder in the Metropolitan Traction Company of Neptune, Saturn, and Venus, and is said to be the moving spirit back of the new underground electric in Hades."

"I guess he'll do," said I, reflecting with admiration upon the wonderful self-rehabilitation of one I had previously regarded as a foolish incompetent.

"You won't have to guess again in this case," said Adonis, dryly. "You've hit it right the very first time."

"Well, tell me about the links, Adonis," said I. "Getting there seems to be an easy matter, but after you get there, how about the course? Is it eighteen holes?"

"It is," said Adonis, "and of proper length, too, and splendidly arranged. You start at the club-house right near the landing-stage and play right around the planet, so that when you're through you're back at the club-house again. At the ninth hole there is a half-way house, where you can get nectar, and ambrosia, and sarsaparilla, and any other soft drink you want."

"No hard drinks, eh?" I queried.

"Not at the half-way house," said Adonis. "We gods have too much sense to indulge in hard drinks in the middle of a game. If you want hard drinks you have to wait till you get back to the club-house."

"That is rather sensible," I said, as I thought of how a Martini cocktail taken at the ninth hole had ruined my chances in the Noodleport Annual Handicap last autumn. "But I say, Adonis," I added, "did I understand you to say that you played all around Mars?"

"Yes - why not?" said he.

"Pretty long holes, I should say," said I. "Mars is four thousand miles round, isn't it?"

"You *are* an earth-worm," he retorted, forgetting his place wholly in his scorn for my picayune ideas. "Calling a paltry four thousand miles long - why, you can play around that links in two hours and a half."

"Indeed?" said I. "And how long may your hours be? Everything here is on such a magnificent scale, I suppose one of your hours is about equal to one of our decades."

"Oh no," said Adonis. "It isn't that way at all. Fact is, we make our hours to suit ourselves. I am merely reckoning on a basis that you would comprehend. I meant two and a half of your hours. Any moderately expert player can play the Mars links in that time. Take the first hole, for instance - it's only two hundred and fifty miles long."

"Really - is that all!" I ejaculated, growing sarcastic. "A drive, two brassies, an approach, and forty puts, I presume?"

"For a duffer, perhaps," retorted Adonis. "Willie Ph[oe]bus does it in six. A seventy-five-mile drive, a seventy-mile brassie, a loft over the canal for twenty-five miles, a forty-five-mile cleak, a thirty-mile approach, and -"

"A dead easy put of five miles!" I put in, making a pretence of being no longer astonished.

"That's the idea," said Adonis. "Of course, everybody can't do it," he added. "And bogie for that hole is really seven. Willie Ph[oe]bus played too well for a gentleman, so we made him a professional. He'll give you lessons for a thousand dollars an hour, if you want him to."

"Thanks," said I. "I'll think about it. Can he teach me how to drive a ball seventy-five miles?"

"That depends on your capacity," said Adonis. "Some of the best players frequently drive seventy-five miles - the record is ninety-six miles, made by Jove himself. Willie taught him."

"For Heaven's sake!" I cried, losing my self-poise for an instant. "What do you drive with? Olympian Gatling guns?"

"Not at all," replied Adonis. "We use one of our regular drivers - the best is called the 'celestial catapult.' Ph[oe]bus sells 'em at the Caddie House for five hundred dollars apiece. If you strike a ball fair and square with the 'celestial catapult,' and neither pull nor slice, it can't help going forty miles, anyhow."

"And how, may I ask, do the caddies find a ball that goes seventy-five miles?"

"They don't have to. All our balls are self-finding," said Adonis. "The ball in use now is a recent invention of Vulcan's. They cost twelve hundred dollars a dozen. They are made of liquefied electricity. We take the electric current, liquefy it, then solidify it, then mould it into the form of a sphere. Inside we place a little gong, that begins to ring as soon as the ball lands. The electricity in it is what makes it fly so rapidly and so far, and even you mortals know the principle of the electric bell."

"Oh, indeed we do," said I, pulling at my mustache nervously. I was beginning to get excited over this celestial golf. On earth I have all of the essentials of a first-class golf maniac, except the ability to play the game. But this so far surpassed anything I had ever seen or imagined before that I was growing too keen over it for comfort. I was in real need of having my spirits curbed, so I ventured to inquire after a phase of the game that has always dampened my ardor in the past - the caddie service. I did not expect that this could attain perfection even in Olympus, and I was not far wrong.

"You must have pretty lively caddies," I threw out.

Adonis sighed. "You'd think so, but that's where we are always in trouble. We've tried various schemes, but they haven't any of 'em worked well. At first we took our own Olympian boys. We got the mother of the Gracchi to lend us her offspring, but they weren't worth a rap. Then we hired forty little devils from Hades, and we had to send them back inside of a week. They were regular little imps. They were cutting up monkey shines all the time, and waggled their horrid little tails so constantly that Jove himself couldn't keep his eye on the ball - and the language they used was something frightful. You couldn't trust them to clean your clubs, because there wasn't any power anywhere that could keep them from running off with 'em; and in the matter of balls, they'd steal every blessed one they could lay their hands on. We finally had to employ cherubs. We've about sixty of 'em on hand now all the time, and they come as near being perfect as you could expect. Ever see a cherub?"

"Only in pictures," said I. "They're just heads with wings, aren't they?"

"Yes," said Adonis, "and, having no bodies, they're seldom in the way, and some of the best of 'em can fly almost as fast as the ball."

"How do they carry the bags?" I asked, much interested.

"They hang 'em about their necks, just above their wings," Adonis explained, "but even they are not perfect. They fly very carelessly, and often, in swooping about the sky, drop your clubs out of the bag and smash 'em; and they all look so infernally alike that you can never tell your own caddy from the other fellow's, which is sometimes very confusing."

"Still," I put in, "a caddie with no pockets is a very safe person to intrust with golf balls."

"That's very true," said Adonis, "and I suppose the cherubs make as good caddies as we can expect. Caddies will be caddies, and that's the end of it. You can't expect a caddie to do just right any more than you can expect water to flow uphill. There are certain immutable laws of the universe which are as unchangeable in Olympus as on earth or in Hades. Ice is cold, fire is hot, water is wet, and caddies are caddies."

"Very true," said I, reflecting upon the ways of "Some Caddies I have Met." "What do you pay them a round?"

"One hundred and twenty-five dollars," said Adonis.

"Cheap enough," said I. "But tell me, Adonis," I continued, "who is your amateur champion?"

"Jupiter, of course," said Adonis, with an impatient shake of his head. "He's champion of everything. It's one of his prerogatives. We don't any of us dare win a cup from him for fear he'll use his power to destroy us. That is one of the features of this Olympian life that is not pleasant - though, for goodness' sake, don't say I told you! He'd send me into perpetual exile if he knew I'd spoken that way. He's threatened to make me Governor-General of the Dipper half a dozen times already for things I've said, and I have to be very careful, or he'll do it."

"An unpleasant post, that?"

"Well," he said, "I don't exactly know how to compare it so that you would understand precisely. I should say, however, it would be about as agreeable as being United States ambassador to Borneo."

"I'll never tell, Adonis," said I, "and I'm very much obliged to you for our pleasant chat. Your description of the links has interested me hugely. If I could afford a game at your prices, I think I'd play."

"Oh, as for that," said Adonis, laughing, "don't let that bother you. Whenever you want to pay a bill here all you have to do is to press the cash button on the teleseme over there, and they'll send the money up from the office."

"But how shall I ever repay the office?" I cried.

"Press the button to the left of it, and they'll send you up a receipt in full," he replied.

"You mean to say that this hotel is run - " I began.

"On the Olympian plan," interrupted the valet with a low bow. "All bills here are of that pleasing variety known as 'Self-paying.'"

With which comforting assurance Adonis left me, and I started for the dining-room, my appetite considerably whetted by the idea of a game of golf over links four thousand miles in length with balls that could be driven fifty or sixty miles, and cherubs for caddies, at no cost to myself whatsoever.

VI

IN THE DINING-ROOM

As I emerged from the door of my room into the hall, I found a small sedan-chair, of highly ornamental make, awaiting my convenience, carried upon the shoulders of two diminutive boys, who were as black, and shone as lustrously, as a bit of highly polished ebony. I had never seen their like before, save in an occasional bit of statuary in Italy, wherein marbles of differing hue and shade had been ingeniously used by the sculptor to give color to his work. The boys themselves, as I have said, were of polished ebony hue, while the breech-cloths which formed their sole garment were of purest alabaster white. Upon their heads were turbans of pink. They grinned broadly as I came out, and opened the door of the chair for me.

"Dis way fo' de dinin'-room, sah," said one of them, showing a set of ivory teeth that dazzled my eyes.

I thanked him and entered the chair. When I was seated, I turned to the little chap.

"What particular god do you happen to be, Sambo?" I asked. It was probably not the most reverent way to put it, but in a community like Olympus gods are really at a discount, and the black particle was so like a small pickaninny I used to know in Savannah that I could not address him as if he were Jupiter himself.

"Massy me, massa," he returned, his smile nearly cutting the top of his head off, reaching as it did around to the back of his ears. "I ain' no gord. I'se jess one o' dese low-down or'nary toters. Me an' him totes folks roun' de hotel."

"A very useful function that, Sambo; and where were you born?" I asked. "North Carolina, or Georgia?"

"Me?" he replied, looking at me quizzically. "I guess yo's on'y foolin', massa. Me? Why, I 'ain't never been borned at all, sah -"

"Jess growed, eh - like Topsy?" I asked.

"Who dat, Topsy?" he demanded.

"Oh, she was a little nigger girl that became very famous," I explained.

"Doan' know nuffin' 'bout no Topsy," he said, shaking his head. "We ain' niggers, eider, yo' know, me an' him ain't. We's statulary."

"What?" I cried. The word seemed new.

"Statulary," he continued. "We was carved, we was. There ain't nothin' borned 'bout us. Never knowed who pap was. Man jess took a lot o' mahble, he did, an' chiselled me an' him out."

I eyed both boys closely and perceived that in all probability he spoke the truth. His flesh and dress had all of the texture of marble, but now the question came up as to the gift of speech and movement and the marvellous and graceful flexibility of their limbs.

"You can't fool me, Sambo," said I. "You're nothing but a very good-looking little nigger. You can't make me believe that you are another Galatea."

"Doan' no nuffin' 'bout no gal's tears," he returned instantly. "But I done tole yo' de truf. Me an' him was chiselled out o' brack marble by pap. Ef we'd been borned we'd been niggahs sho' nuff, but bein' carvin's, like I tole yuh, we's statulary."

"But how does it come that if you are only statuary, you can move about, and talk, and breathe?" I demanded.

"Yo'll have to ask mistah Joop'ter 'bout dat," the boy answered. "He done gave us dese gif's, an' we's a-usin' ob 'em. De way it happened was like o' dis. Me an' him was a standin' upon a petterstal down in one o' dem mahble yards what dey calls gall'ries in Paris. We'd been sent dah by de man what done chiselled us, an' Joop'ter he came 'long wid Miss' Juno an' when he seed us he said: 'Dare you is, Juno! Dem boys'll make mighty good buttonses foh de hotel.' Juno she laffed, an' said dat was so, on'y she couldn't see as we had many buttons. 'Would you like to have 'em?' Joop'ter ast, and she said 'suttinly.' So he tu'ned hisself into a 'Merican millionaire an' bought me an' him off 'n de manager, an' he had us sent here. All dat time we was nuffin' but mahble figgers, but soon's we arrived here, Joop'ter sent us up-stairs to de lab'ratory, an' fust ting me an' him knowed we was livin' bein's."

I admired Jupiter's taste, not failing either to marvel at the wonderful power which only once before, as far as I knew, he had exerted to give to a bit of sculpture all the flush and glory of life, as in the case set forth in the pathetic tale of Pygmalion and Galatea.

"And does he do this sort of thing often?" I inquired.

"Yass indeedy," said Sambo. "He's doin' it all de time. Mos' ob de help in dis hotel is statulary, an' ef yo' wants to see a reel lively time 'foh yo' goes back home, go to de Zoo an' see 'em feed de Trojan Hoss, an' de Cardiff Giant. He brang bofe dem freaks to life, an' now he can't get rid ob 'em. Dat Trojan Hoss suttinly am a berry debbil. He stans up gentle as a lamb tell he gets about a hundred an' fifty people inside o' him, an' den he p'tends like he's gwine to run away, an' he cyanters, an' cyanters aroun', tell ebberybody's dat seasick dey can't res'."

I resolved then and there to see the Trojan Horse, but not to get inside of him. I never before had suspected that the famous beast had a sense of humor in his makeup. I was about to make some further inquiry when a bell above us began to sound forth sonorously.

"Massy me!" cried little Sambo, springing to his place in front of the chair. "Dat's de third an' lass call for breakfas'. We done spent too much time talkin'."

With which observation, he and his companion, shouldering their burden, trotted along the richly furnished hall to the dining-room. I then observed a charming feature of life in the Olympian Hotel, and I presume it obtains elsewhere in that favored spot. There are no such things as stairs within its walls. From the magnificent office on the ground floor to the glorious dining-room on the forty-eighth, the broad corridor runs round and round and round again with an upward incline that is barely perceptible - indeed, not perceptible at all either to the eye or to the muscles of the leg. And while there are the most speedy elevators connecting all the various floors, one can, if one chooses, walk from cellar to roof of this marvellous place without realizing that he is mounting to an unusual elevation. And in the evening these corridors form a magnificent parade, brilliantly lighted, upon which are to be met all the wealth, beauty, and fashion of Olympus - alas! that I have no means of returning there with certain of my friends with whom I would share the good things that have come into my life!

But to return to the story. Sambo and his brother soon "toted" me to the entrance of the dining-room - graceful little beggars they were, too.

"Your breakfast is ready, sir," said the head waiter, bowing low.

What impelled me to do so I shall never know, but it was an inspiration. I seemed to recognize the man at once, and, as I had frequently done on earth to my own advantage, I addressed him by name.

"Having a good season, Memnon?" I said, slipping a silver dollar into his hand.

It worked. Whether I should have found the same excellent service had I not spoken pleasantly to him I, of course, cannot say, but I have never been so well cared for elsewhere. The captious reader may ask how anything so essentially worldly as a silver dollar ever crept into Olympus. I can only say that one of the magic properties of the garment I wore was that whatever I put my hand into my pocket for, I got. As a travelled American, realizing the potency under similar conditions of that heavy and ugly coin, I instinctively sought for it in my pocket and it was there. I do not attempt to explain the process of its getting there. It suffices to say that, as the guest of the gods, my every wish was met with speedy attainment. I could not help but marvel, too, at the appropriateness of everything. What better than that the King of the Ethiopians should be head waiter to the gods!

"Things are never dull here, sir," said Memnon, pocketing my dollar and escorting me to my table. "We do not often have visitors like yourself, however, and we are very glad to see you."

I sat down before a magnificent window which seemed to open out upon a universe hitherto undreamed of.

"Do you wish the news, sir?" Memnon asked, respectfully.

"Yes," said I. "Ah - news from home, Memnon," I added.

"Political or merely family?" said he.

"Family," said I.

Memnon busied himself about the window and in a moment, gazing through it, I had the pleasure of seeing my two boys eating their supper and challenging each other to mortal combat over a delinquent strawberry resting upon the tablecloth.

"Give me a little politics, Memnon," said I, as the elder boy thrashed the younger, not getting the strawberry, however, which in a quick moment, between blows, the younger managed to swallow. "They seem to be about as usual at home."

And I was immediately made aware of the intentions of the administration at Washington merely by looking through a window. There were the President and his cabinet and - some others who assist in making up the mind of the statesman.

"Now a dash of crime," said I.

"High or low?" asked Memnon, fingering the push-button alongside of the window.

"The highest you've got," said I.

I shall not describe what I saw. It was not very horrible. It was rather discouraging. It dealt wholly with the errors of what is known as Society. It showed the mistakes of persons for whom I had acquired a feeling of awe. It showed so much that I summoned Memnon to shut the glass off. I was really afraid somebody else might see. And I did not wish to lose my respect for people who were leaders in the highest walks of social life. Still, a great many things that have happened since in high life have not been wholly surprising to me. I have furthermore so ordered my own goings and comings since that time that I have no fear of what the Peeping Toms of Olympus may see. If mankind could only be made to understand that this window of Olympus opens out upon every act of their lives, there might be radical reforms in some quarters where it would do a deal of good, although to the general public there seems to be no need for it.

At this point a waiter put a small wafer about as large as a penny upon the table.

"H'm - what's that, Memnon?" I asked.

"Essence of melon," said he.

"Good, is it?" I queried.

"You might taste it and see, sir," he said, with a smile. "It is one of a lot especially prepared for Jupiter."

I put the thing in my mouth, and oh, the sensation that followed! I have eaten melons, and I have dreamed melons, but never in either experience was there to be found such an ecstasy of taste as I now got.

"Another, Memnon - another!" I cried.

"If you wish, sir," said he. "But very imprudent, sir. That wafer was constructed from six hundred of the choicest - "

"Quite right," said I, realizing the situation; "quite right. Six hundred melons *are* enough for any man. What do you propose to give me now?"

"*Oeufs Midas*," said Memnon.

"Sounds rather rich," I observed.

"It would cost you 4,650,000 francs for a half portion at a Paris cafe, if you could get it there - which you can't."

"And what, Memnon," said I, "is the peculiarity of eggs *Midas*?"

"It's nothing but an omelet, sir," he replied; "but it is made of

John Kendrick Bangs

eggs laid by the goose of whom you have probably read in the *Personal Recollections of Jack the Giant-Killer*. They are solid gold."

"Heavens!" I cried. "Solid gold! Great Scott, Memnon, I can't digest a solid gold omelet. What do you think I am - an assay office?"

Memnon grinned until every tooth in his head showed, making his mouth look like the keyboard of a grand piano.

"It is perfectly harmless the way it is prepared in the kitchen, sir," he explained. "It isn't an eighteen-karat omelet, as you seem to think. The eggs are solid, but the omelet is not. It is, indeed, only six karats fine. The alloy consists largely of lactopeptine, hydrochloric acid, and various other efficient digestives which render it innocuous to the most delicate digestion."

"Very well, Memnon," I replied, making a wry face, "bring it on. I'll try a little of it, anyhow." I must confess it did not sound inviting, but a guest should never criticise the food that is placed before him. My politeness was well repaid, for nothing more delicate in the way of an omelet has ever titillated my palate. There was a slight metallic taste about it at first, but I soon got over that, just as I have got used to English oysters, which, when I eat them, make me feel for a moment as if I had bitten off the end of a brass door-knob; and had I not calculated the cost, I should have asked for a second helping.

Memnon then brought me a platter containing a small object that looked like a Hamburg steak, and a most delicious cup of *cafe au lait*.

"Filet Olympus," he observed, "and coffee direct from the dairy of the gods."

Both were a joy.

"Never tasted such a steak!" I said, as the delicate morsel actually melted like butter in my mouth.

"No, sir, you never did," Memnon agreed. "It is cut from the steer bred for the sole purpose of supplying Jupiter and his family with tenderloin. We take the calf when it is very young, sir, and surround it with all the luxuries of a bovine existence. It is fed on the most delicate fodder, especially prepared by chemists under the direction of AEsculapius. The cattle, instead of toughening their muscles by walking to pasture, are waited upon by cow-boys in livery. A gentle amount of exercise, just enough to keep them in condition, is taken at regular hours every day, and at night they are put to sleep in feather beds and covered with eiderdown quilts at seven o'clock."

"Don't they rebel?" I asked. "I should think a moderately active calf would be hard to manage that way."

"Oh, at first a little, but after a while they come to like it, and by the time they are ready for killing they are as tender as humming birds' tongues," said Memnon. "If you take him young enough, you can do almost anything you like with a calf."

It seemed like a marvellous scheme, and far more humane than that of fattening geese for the sale of their livers.

"And this coffee, Memnon? You said it was fresh from the dairy of the gods. You get your coffee from the dairy?" I asked.

"The breakfast coffee - yes, sir," replied Memnon. "Fresh every morning. You must ask the steward to let you see the *cafe-au-lait* herd -"

"The what?" I demanded.

"The *cafe-au-lait herd*," repeated Memnon. "A special permit is required to go through the coffee pasture where these cows are fed. Some one, who had a grudge against Pales, who is in charge of the dairymaids, got into the field one night and sowed a lot of chicory in with the coffee, and the result was that the next season we got the worst coffee from those cows you ever tasted. So they made a rule that no one is allowed to go there any more without a card from the steward."

"You don't mean to say -" I began.

"Yes, I do," said Memnon. "It is true. We pasture our cows on a coffee farm, and, instead of milk, we get this that you are drinking."

"Wonderful idea!" said I.

"It is, indeed," said Memnon; "that is, from your point of view. From ours, it does not seem so strange. We are used to marvels here, sir," he continued. "Would you care for anything more, sir?"

"No, Memnon," said I. "I have fared sumptuously - my - ah - my appetite is somewhat taken away by all these tremendous things."

"I will have an appetite up for you, if you wish," he replied, simply, as if it were the easiest thing in the world.

"No, thank you," said I. "I think I'll wait until I am acclimated. I never eat heavily for the first twenty-four hours when I am in a strange place."

And with this I went to the door, feeling, I must confess, a trifle ill. The steak and coffee were all right, but there was a suggestion of pain in my right side. I could not make up my mind if it were the six hundred melons or whether a nugget from the omelet had got caught in my vermiform appendix.

At any rate, I didn't wish to eat again just then.

At the door the sedan-chair and the two little blackamoors were awaiting me.

"We have orders to take you to the Zoo, sah," said Sambo.

"All right, Sambo," said I. "I'm all ready. A little air will do me good."

And we moved along.

I forgot to mention that, as he closed the chair door upon me, Memnon handed me back the silver dollar I had given him.

"What is this, Memnon?" said I.

"The dollar you wished me to keep for you, sir," he replied.

"But I intended it for you," said I.

His face flushed.

"I am just as much obliged, sir, but, really, I couldn't, you know. We don't take tips in Olympus, sir."

"Indeed?" said I. "Well - I'm sorry to have offended you, Memnon. I meant it all right. Why didn't you tell me when I gave it you?"

"I should have given you a check for it, sir. I supposed you didn't wish to carry anything so heavy about with you."

"Ah!" said I, replacing the dollar in my pocket. "Thank you for your care of it, Memnon. No offence, I hope?"

"None at all, sir," he replied, again showing his wonderful ivory teeth. "I don't take offence at anything so trifling. Had you handed me a billion dollars, I should have declined to wait on you."

And he bowed me away in a fashion which made me feel keenly the narrowness of my escape.

VII

AESCULAPIUS, M.D.

We had not gone very far along when the pain in my side became poignant and I called out of the window to Sambo:

"Sammy, is there a doctor anywhere on the way out to the Zoo?" I asked.

"Yassir," he replied, slowing down a trifle. "We gotter go right by de doh ob Dr. Skilapius."

"Doctor who?" I asked - the name was new to me.

"'Tain't *Skill*-apius," growled the boy behind, who seemed rather jealous that I had taken no notice of him. "It's Eee-skill-apius."

"Oh," said I, beginning to catch their drift. "Dr. AEsculapius. Is that what you are trying to say?"

"Yassir," said both boys. "Dass de man."

"Well, stop at his office a moment," said I. "I'm feeling a trifle ill."

In a few minutes we drew up before a large door to the right of the corridor before which there hung a shingle marked in large gilt letters:

AESCULAPIUS, M.D.

Office Hours: 10 to 12.

Tuesdays.

I knocked at the door and was promptly admitted.

"I wish to see the doctor," said I.

"This is Monday, sir," the maid replied - I couldn't quite place her, but she seemed rather above her station and was stunningly beautiful.

"What of that?" I demanded, as fiercely as I could, considering how pretty the maid was.

"The doctor can only be seen on Tuesdays," said she. "It's on the door."

"But I'm sick," I cried. "Very sick, indeed."

"No doubt," she replied, with a shrug of her shoulders that I found very fetching. "Else you would not have come. But you are not so sick that you can't wait until to-morrow, or if you are, you might as well die, because the doctor won't take a case he can't think over a week."

"Nice arrangement, that," said I, scornfully. "It may do very well for immortals, but for a mortal it's pretty poor business."

The maid's manner underwent an immediate change.

"Excuse me, sir," she said, making me a courtesy. "I did not know you were a mortal. I presumed you were a minor god. The doctor will see you at once."

I was ushered into the consulting-room immediately - in fact, too quickly. I wanted to thank the pretty maid for taking me for an immortal. There was no time for this, however, for in a moment AEsculapius himself appeared.

"You must pardon Alcestis," he said, after the first greetings were over. "She is new to the business and doesn't know a god from a hole in the ground. She presumed you were immortal and did not realize the emergency."

"That's all right, doctor," said I, glad to learn who the entrancing person at the door was. "I've called to see you because -"

"Pray be silent," the doctor interrupted, holding his hand up in admonition. "Let me discover your symptoms for myself. It is the surer method. Physicians in your world are frequently led astray by placing too much reliance upon what their patients tell them. I have devised a new system. *Believe nothing the patient says.* See? If a man tells me he has a headache, I send him to a chiropodist. If his ankle pains him, I send him to an oculist. If he says his chest is oppressed, I have him treated for spinal meningitis; and an alleged pain in the back my assistants cure by placing a mustard plaster on the throat."

"Then your medical principles are based on what, doctor?" I asked, somewhat amused.

"A simple motto which prevails among you mortals: 'All men are liars' - 'Omnes homines mendaces sunt.' It is safer than your accepted methods below. A sick man is the last man in the universe to describe his symptoms accurately. The mere fact that he is ill distorts his judgment. Therefore, I never allow it. If I can't find out for myself what is the matter with a patient, I give up the case."

"And the patient dies?" I suggested.

"Not if he is an immortal," he replied, quietly. "Come over

John Kendrick Bangs

here," he added, indicating a spot near the window where there was a strong light. I went, and AEsculapius, taking a pair of eye-glasses from a cabinet in one corner of his apartment, placed them on the bridge of his nose.

"Now look out of the window," said he. "To the left."

I obeyed at once. What I saw may not be described. I shrank back in horror, for I saw so much real suffering that my own trouble grew less in intensity.

"Now look me straight in the eye," said AEsculapius, an amused smile playing about his lips.

I turned my vision straight upon his glasses and was abashed. I averted my glance.

"Nonsense," said he, taking me by the shoulders. "Look at my pupils - straight - don't be afraid - there! That's it. These glasses won't hurt you, and, after all, I'm not very terrible," he added, genially.

It required an effort, but I made it, although, in so doing, I seemed to be turning my soul inside out for his inspection.

"H'm," breathed AEsculapius. "Rather serious. You think you have appendicitis."

"Have I?" I cried.

AEsculapius laughed. "*Have* you?" he asked. "What do you think you think?"

"I think I have," said I, my heart growing faint at the very thought I thought I was thinking.

"You are at least sure of your convictions," said AEsculapius. "Now, as a matter of fact, the thoughts your thoughtful nature has induced you to think are utterly valueless. You have a pain in your side?"

"Yes," said I. "And a very painful pain in my side - and I am not putting on any side in my pain either," I added.

"No doubt," said AEsculapius. "But are you sure it is in your side, or isn't it your chest that aches a trifle, eh?"

"Not much," said I, growing doubtful on the subject.

"Still it aches," said he.

"Yes," I answered, the pain in my side weakening in favor of one in my chest. "It does." And it really did, like the deuce.

"Now about that pain in your chest," said AEsculapius. "Isn't it rather higher up - in your throat, instead of your chest?"

My throat began to hurt, and abominably. Every particle of it throbbed with pain, and my chest was immediately relieved.

"I think," said I, weakly, "that the pain *is* rather in my throat than in my chest."

"But your side doesn't ache at all?" suggested AEsculapius.

I had forgotten my side altogether.

"Not a bit," said I; and it didn't.

"So far, so good," said the doctor. "Now, my friend, about this throat trouble of yours. Do you think you have diphtheria, or merely toothache?"

I hadn't thought of toothache before, but as soon as the doctor mentioned it, a pang went through my lower jaw, and my larynx seemed all right again.

"Well, doctor," said I, "as a matter of fact, the pain does seem

John Kendrick Bangs

to be in my wisdom teeth."

"So-called," said he, quietly. "More tooth than wisdom, generally. And not in your throat?" continued the doctor.

"Not a bit of it," said I. My throat seemed strong enough for a political campaign in which I was principal speaker. "It's *all* in my teeth."

"Upper or lower?" he asked, with a laugh, and then he gazed fixedly at me.

I had not realized that I had upper teeth until he spoke, and a shudder went through me as a semicircle of pain shot through my upper jaw.

"Upper," I retorted, with some surliness.

"Verging a trifle on your cheekbones, and thence to the optic nerve," he said, calmly, still gazing into my soul. "I'll try your sight. Look at that card over there, and tell me - "

"What nonsense is this, doctor?" I cried, angry at his airy manner and manifest control over my symptoms. "There is nothing the matter with my eyes. They're as good as any one of the million eyes of your friend the Argus."

"Then what, in the name of Jupiter, is the matter with you?" he ejaculated, elevating his eyebrows.

"Nothing at all," said I, sulkily.

AEsculapius threw himself on the sofa and roared with laughter.

"Perfectly splendid!" he said, when he had recovered from his mirth. "Perfectly splendid! You are the best example of the value of my system I've had in a long time. Now let me show you something," he added. "Put these glasses on."

He took the glasses from his nose and put them astride of mine, and lead me before a mirror - a cheval-glass arrangement that stood in one corner of the room.

"Now look yourself straight in the eye," said he.

I did so, and truly it was as if I looked upon the page of a book printed in the largest and clearest type. I hesitate to say what I saw written there, since the glass was strong enough to reach not only the mind itself, but further into the very depths of my subself-consciousness. On the surface, man thinks well of himself; this continues in modified intensity to his self-consciousness, but the fool does not live who, in his subself-consciousness, the Holy of Holies of Realization, does not know that he is a fool.

"Take 'em off," I cried, for they seemed to burn into the very depths of my soul.

"That isn't necessary," said AEsculapius, kindly. "Just turn your eyes away from the glass a moment and they won't bother you. I want to cure this trouble of yours."

I stopped looking at myself in the mirror and the tense condition of my nerves was immediately relieved.

"Feel better right away, eh?" he asked.

"Yes," I admitted.

"So I thought," he said. "You've momentarily given up self-contemplation. Now lower your gaze. Look at your chest a moment."

Just what were the properties of the glass I do not know, nor do I know how one's chest should look, but, as I looked down, I found that just as I could penetrate to the depths of my mind through my eyes, so was it possible for me to inspect myself physically.

"Nothing the matter there, eh?" said AEsculapius.

"Not that I can see," said I.

"Nor I," said he. "Now, if you think there is anything the matter with you anywhere else," he added, "you are welcome to use the glasses as long as you see fit."

I took a sneaking glance at my right side and was immediately made aware of the fact that all was well with me there, and that all my trouble had come from my ill-advised "wondering" whether that Midas omelet would bother me or not.

"These glasses are wonderful," said I.

"They are a great help," said AEsculapius.

"And do you always permit your patients to put them on?" I asked.

"Not always," said he. "Sometimes people really have something the matter with them. More often, of course, they haven't. It would never do to let a really sick man see his condition. If they are ill, I can see at once what is the matter by means of these spectacles, and can, of course, prescribe. If they are not, there is no surer means of effecting a cure than putting these on the patient's nose and letting him see for himself that he is all right."

"They have all the quality of the X-ray light," I suggested, turning my gaze upon an iron safe in the corner of the room, which immediately disclosed its contents.

"They are X-ray glasses," said AEsculapius. "In a good light you can see through anything with 'em on. I have lenses of the same kind in my window, and when you came up I looked at you through the window-pane and saw at once that there was nothing the matter with you."

"I wish our earthly doctors had glasses like these," I ventured, taking them off, for truly I was beginning to fancy a strain.

"They have - or at least they have something quite as good," said AEsculapius. "They are all my disciples, and in the best instances they can see through the average patient without them. They have insight. You don't believe you deceive your physician, do you?"

"I have sometimes thought so," said I, not realizing the trap the doctor was setting.

"How foolish!" he cried. "Why should you wish to?"

I was covered with confusion.

"Never mind," said AEsculapius, smiling pleasantly. "You are only human and cannot help yourself. It is your imagination leads you astray. Half the time when you send for your physician there is nothing the matter with you."

"He always prescribes," I retorted.

"That is for your comfort, not his," said AEsculapius, firmly.

"And sometimes they operate when it isn't necessary," I put in, persistently.

"True," said AEsculapius. "Very true. Because if they didn't, the patient would die of worry."

"Humph!" said I, incredulous. "I never knew that the operation for appendicitis was a mind cure."

"It is - frequently," observed the doctor. "There are more people, my friend, who have appendicitis on their minds than there are those who have it in their vermiforms. Don't forget that."

It was a revelation, and, to tell the truth, it has been a revelation of comfort ever since.

"I fancy, doctor," said I, after a pause, "that you are a Christian Scientist. All troubles are fanciful and indicative of a perverse soul."

AEsculapius flushed.

"If one of the gods had said that," he replied, "I should have operated upon him. As a mortal, you are privileged to say unpleasant things, just as a child may say things to his elders with impunity which merit extreme punishment. Christian Science is all right when you are truly well - in good physical condition. It is a sure cure for imaginary troubles, but when you are really sick, it is not of Olympus, but of Hades."

AEsculapius spoke with all the passion of a mortal, and I was embarrassed. "I did not mean to say anything unpleasant, doctor," said I.

"That's all right, my lad," said AEsculapius, patting me on the back. "I knew that. If I hadn't known it, you'd have been on the table by this time. And now, good-bye. Curb your imagination. Think about others. Don't worry about yourself without cause, and never send for a doctor unless you know there's something wrong. If I had my way you mortals would be deprived of imagination. That is your worst disease, and if at any time you wish yours amputated, come to me and I'll fix you out."

"Thanks, doctor," I replied; "but I don't think I'll accept your offer, because I need my imagination in my business."

And then, realizing that I had received my *conge*, I prepared to depart.

"How much do I owe you, doctor?" I asked, putting my hand into the pocket of my gown, confident of finding whatever I should need.

"Nothing," said he. "The real physician can never be paid. He either restores your health or he does not. If he restores your health, he saves your life, and he is entitled to what your life is worth. If he does not restore your health - he has failed, and is entitled to nothing. All you have will never pay your doctor for what he does for you. Therefore, go in peace."

I stood abashed in the presence of this wise man, and, as I went forth from his office, I realized the truth of what he had said. In our own world we place a value upon the service of the man who carries us over the hard and the dark places. Yet who can really repay him for all that he does for us when by his skill alone we are rescued from peril?

I re-entered my sedan-chair and set the blackies off again, with something potent in my mind - how much I truly owed to the good man who has taken at times the health of my children, of my wife, of myself, in his hands and has seen us safely through to port. I have not yet been able to estimate it, but if ever he reads these lines, he will know that I pay him in gratitude that which the world with all its wealth cannot give.

"Now for the Zoo, boys," I cried. "AEsculapius has fixed me up."

And we scampered on.

VIII

AT THE ZOO

We had not travelled far from the office of AEsculapius when my little carriers turned from the broad and beautiful corridor into a narrow passage, through which they proceeded with some difficulty until we reached the other side of this strangely constructed home of the gods. As we emerged into the light of day, the view that presented itself was indescribably beautiful. I have looked from our own hills at home upon many a scene of grandeur. From the mountain peaks of New Hampshire, with the sun streaming down upon me, I have looked upon the valleys beneath through rifts in clouds that had not ventured so high, and were drenching the glorious green below with refreshing rains, and have stood awed in the presence of one of the simplest moods of nature. But the sight that greeted my eyes as I passed along that exterior road of Olympus, under the genial auspices of those wonderful gods, appealed to something in my soul which had never before been awakened, and which I shall never be able adequately to describe. The mere act of seeing seemed to be uplifting, and, from the moment I looked downward upon the beloved earth, I ceased to wonder that gods were godlike - indeed, my real wonder was that they were not more so. It seemed difficult to believe that there was anything earthly about earth. The world was idealized even to myself, who had never held it to be a bad sort of place. There were rich pastures, green to the most soul-satisfying degree, upon which cattle fed and lived their lives of content; here and there were the great cities of earth seen through a haze that softened all their roughness; nothing sordid appeared; only the fair side of life was visible.

And I began to see how it came about that these Olympian gods had lost control over man. If the world, with all its joys and all its miseries, presents to the controlling power merely its joyous side, what sympathy can one look for in one's deity? There was Paris and Notre Dame in the sunlight. But the Morgue at the back of Notre Dame - in the shadow of its sunlit towers - that was not visible to the eye of the casual god who drove his blackamoors along that entrancing roadway. There was London and the inspiring pile of Westminster showing up its majestic top, lit by the wondrous light of the sun - but still undiscovered of the gods there rolled on its farther side the Thames, dark as the Styx, a very grave of ambition, yet the last solace of many a despairing soul. London Bridge may tell the gods of much that may not be seen from that glorious driveway along the exterior of Olympus.

I found myself growing maudlin, and I pulled myself together.

"Magnificent view, Sammy," said I.

"Yassir," he replied, trotting along faithfully. "Dass what dey all says. *I* 'ain't nebber seen it. 'Ain't got time to look at it."

"Well, stop a moment and look," said I. "Isn't it magnificent?"

The blackies stopped and looked.

"Putty good," said Sammy, "but I doan' care fo' views," he added. "Dey makes me dizzy."

I gave Sammy up from that moment. He was well carved, a work of art, in fact, but he was essentially modern, and I was living in the antique.

"Hustle along to the Zoo," I cried, with some impatience, and I was truly "hustled."

"Here we is," said Sammy, settling down on his haunches at the end of a five-mile trot. "Dis is it."

We had stopped before a gate not entirely unlike those the Japanese erect before popular places of amusement they frequent.

I descended from the chair and was greeted by an attendant who demanded to know what I wished to see.

"The animals," said I.

He laughed. "Well," he said, "I'll show you what I've got, but truly most of them have gone off on vacation."

"Is the Trojan Horse here?" I demanded.

"No," said he. "He's in the repair shop. One of his girders is loose, and the hinges on his door rusted and broke last week. His interior needs painting, and his left hind-leg has been wobbly for a long time. It was really dangerous to keep him longer without repairs."

I was much disappointed. In visiting the Olympian Zoo I was largely impelled by a desire to see the Trojan Horse and compare him with the Coney Island Elephant, which, with the summer hotels of New Jersey and the Statue of Liberty, at that time dominated the minor natural glories of the American coast in the eyes of passengers on in-coming steamships. I think I should even have ventured a ride in his capacious interior despite what Sammy had said of his friskiness and the peril of his action to persons susceptible to sea-sickness.

"Too bad," said I, swallowing my disappointment as best I could. "Still, you have other attractions. How about the Promethean vulture? Is he still living?"

"Unfortunately, no," said the attendant. "He was taken out last year and killed. Got too proud to live. He put in a complaint about his food. Said Prometheus was a very interesting man, but as a diet he was monotonous and demanded a more diversified *menu*. Said he'd like to try Apollo and a Muse or two, for a little while, and preferred Cupids on toast for Sunday-night tea."

"What a vulturian vulture!" said I.

"Wasn't he?" laughed the attendant. "We replied by wringing his neck, and served him up in a chicken salad to a party of tourists from Hades."

This struck me as reasonable, and I said so.

"Well, whatever you happen to have on hand will satisfy me," I added. "Just let me see what animals you have and I'll be content."

"Very well," replied the attendant. "Step this way."

He took me along a charming pathway bordered with many a beautiful tree and adorned with numerous flowers of wondrous fragrance.

"This path is not without interest," he said; "all the trees and shrubs have a history. That laurel over there, for instance, used to be a Daphne. She and Jupiter had a row and he planted her over there. Makes a very pretty tree, eh?"

"Extremely," said I. "Have you many similar ventures?"

"Oh yes. Our botanical gardens are full of them," he replied. "Those trees to the right are Baucis and Philemon. That lotos plant on the left used to be Dryope, and when Adonis isn't busy valeting at the hotel, he comes down here and blooms as an anemone, into which, as you are probably aware, he was changed by Venus. That pink thing by the fountain is Hyacinthus, and over there by the pond is where Narcissus blooms. He's a barber in his off hours."

I had already learned that, so expressed no surprise.

"That's a stunning sunflower you have," I ventured, pointing to a perfect specimen thereof directly ahead of us.

"Yes," said the attendant. "That's Clytie. She's only potted. We don't set her out permanently, because the royal family like to have her on the table at state dinners. And she, poor girl, rather enjoys it. Apollo is generally to be found at these dinners either as a guest or playing a zither or a banjo behind a screen. Wherever he is, the sunflower turns and it affords considerable amusement among Jupiter's guests to watch it. Jupiter has christened Clytie the Sherlock Holmes of Olympus, because wherever Apollo is she spots him. Sometimes when he isn't present, he has to be very careful in his statements about where he has been, for long habit has made Clytie unerring in her instinct."

This seemed to me to be a rather good revenge on Apollo for his very ungodlike treatment of Clytie, and if half the attendant told me that day at the Zoo is true, this excessively fickle Olympian is probably sorry by this time that he treated her originally with such uncalled for disdain.

"Come over here and see the bear-pit," said the guide. I obeyed with alacrity, and, leaning over the rail, had the pleasure of seeing the most beautiful bruin my eyes had ever rested upon. She was as glossy as a new silk hat; her eyes were as soft and timid as those of a frightened deer, and, when she moved, she was the perfection of grace.

"Good-morning, Callisto," said my guide.

"Same to you, my dear Cephalus," the bear returned, in a sweet feminine voice that entranced me.

"How are things with you to-day?" asked Cephalus, with a kindly smile.

"Oh, I can't growl," laughed Callisto - it was evident that the unfortunate woman was not taking her misfortune too seriously. "Only I wish you'd tell people who come here that while I undoubtedly am a bear, I have not yet lost my womanly taste, and I don't want to be fed all the time on buns. If anybody asks you what you think I'd like, tell them that an occasional *omelette soufflee*, or an oyster pate, or a platter of *petits fours* would please me greatly."

"I shall do it, Callisto," said the keeper, as he started to move away. "Meanwhile, here's a stick of chewing-gum for you." Callisto received it with a manifestation of delight which moved me greatly, and I bethought myself of the magic properties of my coat, and plunging my hand into its capacious pockets, I found there an oyster pate that made my mouth water, and an *omelette soufflee* that looked as if it had been made by a Parisian milliner, it was so dainty.

"If madam will permit me," said I, with a bow to Callisto.

"Thank you kindly," the bear replied, in that same thrillingly sweet voice, and dancing with joy. "You are a dear, good man, and if you ever have an enemy, let me know and I'll hug him to death."

As we again turned to go, Cephalus laughed. "Queer case that!" he said. "You'd have thought Juno would let up on that poor woman, but she doesn't for a little bit."

"Well - a jealous woman, my dear Cephalus - "

"True," said he. "That's all true enough, but, great Heavens, man, Juno ought to be used to it by this time with a husband like Jupiter. She's overstocked this Zoo a dozen times already with her jealous freaks, and Jupiter hasn't reformed once. What good does it do?"

"Doesn't she ever let 'em off?" I asked. "Doesn't Callisto ever have a Sunday out, for instance?"

"Yes, but always as a bear, and the poor creature doesn't dare take her chance with the other wild beasts - the real ones. She's just as afraid of bears as she ever was, and if she sees a plain, every-day cow coming towards her, she runs shrieking back to her pit again."

"Poor Callisto," said I. "And Actaeon? How about him?"

"He's here - but he's a holy terror," replied Cephalus, shaking his head. "He gets loose once in a while, and then everybody has to look out for himself, and frankly," Cephalus added, his voice sinking to a whisper, "I don't blame him. Diana treated him horribly."

"I always thought so," said I. "He really wasn't to blame."

"Certainly not," observed Cephalus. "If people will go in swimming out-of-doors, it's their own fault if chance wayfarers stumble upon them. To turn a man into a stag and then set his own dogs on him for a thing he couldn't help strikes me as rank injustice."

"Wonder to me that Jupiter doesn't interfere in this business," said I. "He could help Callisto out without much trouble."

"The point about that is that he's afraid," Cephalus explained. "Juno has threatened to sue him for divorce if he does, and he doesn't dare brave the scandal."

We had by this time reached a long, low building that looked like a stable, and, as we entered, Cephalus observed:

"This is our fire-proof building where we keep our inflammable beasts. That big, sleeping creature that looks like a mastodon lizard is the dragon that your friend St. George, of London, got the best of, and sent here with his compliments. I'll give the beast a prod and let you see how he works."

Cephalus was as good as his word, and for a moment I wished

he wasn't. Such a din as that which followed the dragon's awakening I never heard before, and every time the horrible beast opened his jaws it was as if a fire-works factory had exploded.

"Very dangerous creature that," said Cephalus. "But he is splendid for fetes. Shows off beautifully in the dark. I'll prod him again and just you note the prismatic coloring of his flames. Get up there, Fido," he added, poking the dragon with his stick a second time. "Wake up, and give the gentleman an illumination."

The scene of the moment before was repeated, only with greater intensity, and even in the sunlight I could see that the various hues his fiery breathings took on were gorgeous beyond description. A bonfire built of red, pink, green, and yellow lights, backed up by driftwood in a fearful state of combustion, about describes it.

"Superb," said I, nearly overcome by the grandeur of the scene.

"Well, just imagine it on a dark night!" cried Cephalus, enthusiastically. "Fido is very popular as a living firework, but he's a costly luxury."

I laughed. "Costly?" said I. "I don't see why. Fireworks as grand as that must cost a deal more than he does."

"You don't know," said Cephalus, pressing his lips together. "Why, that dragon eats ten tons of cannel coal a day, and it takes the combined efforts of six stokers, under the supervision of an expert engineer, to keep his appetite within bounds. You never saw such an eater, and as for drinking - well, he's awful. He drinks sixteen gallons of kerosene at luncheon."

I eyed Cephalus narrowly, but beyond a wink at the dragon, I saw no reason to believe that he was deceiving me.

"Then he sets fire to things, and altogether he's an expensive beast Aren't you, Fido?"

"Yep," barked the dragon.

"Now, over there," continued the guide, patting the dragon on the head, whereat the fearful beast wagged his tail and breathed a thousand pounds of steam from his nostrils to express his pleasure. "Over there are the fire-breathing bulls - all the animals here are fire-breathing. The bulls give us a lot of trouble. You can't feed 'em on coal, because their teeth are not strong enough to chew it; and you can't feed 'em on hay, because they'd set fire to it the minute they breathed on it; and you can't put 'em out to pasture because they'd wither up a sixty-acre lot in ten minutes. It's an actual fact that we have to send for Jason three times a day to come here and feed them. He's the only person about who can do it, and how he does it no one knows. He pats them on the neck, and they stop breathing fire. That's all we know."

"But they must eat something. What does Jason give them?" I demanded.

"We've had to invent a food for them," said Cephalus. "Dr. AEsculapius did it. It's a solution of hay, clover, grass, and paraffine mixed with asbestos."

"Paraffine?" I cried. "Why, that's extremely inflammable."

"So are the bulls," was Cephalus's rejoinder. "They counteract each other." I gazed at the animals with admiration. They were undoubtedly magnificent beasts, and they truly breathed fire. Their nostrils suggested the flames that are emitted from the huge naphtha jets that are used to light modern circuses in country towns, and as for their mouths, any one who can imagine a bull with a pair of gas-logs illuminating his reflective smile, instead of teeth, may gain a comprehensive idea of the picture that confronted me.

I had hardly finished looking at these, when Cephalus,

impatient to be through with me, as guides often are with tourists, observed:

"There is the ph[oe]nix."

I turned instantly. I have always wished to see the ph[oe]nix. A bird having apparently the attractive physique of a broiler deliberately sitting on a bonfire had appealed strongly to my interest as well as to my appetite.

"Dear me!" said I. "He's not handsome, is he?"

He was not; resembling an ordinary buzzard with wings outstretched sitting upon that kind of emberesque fire that induces a man in a library to think mournfully about the past, and convinces him - alas! - that if he had the time he could write immortal poetry.

"Not very!" Cephalus acquiesced. "Still, he's all right in a Zoo. He's queer. Look at his nest, if you don't believe it."

"I never believed otherwise, my dear Cephalus," said I. "He seems to me to be a unique thing in poultry. If he were a chicken he would be hailed with delight in my country. A self-broiling broiler - !"

The idea was too ecstatic for expression.

"Well, he isn't a chicken, so your rhapsody doesn't go," said Cephalus. "He's little short of a buzzard. Useful, but not appetizing. If I were a profane mortal, I should call him a condemned nuisance. Most birds build their own nests, and a well-built nest lasts them a whole season. This infernal bird has to have a furnace-man to make his bed for him night and morning, and if, by some mischance, the fire goes out, as fires will do in the best-regulated families, he begins to squawk, and he squawks, and he squawks, and he squawks until the keeper comes and sets his nest a-blazing again. He has a voice like a sick fog-horn that drives everybody crazy."

John Kendrick Bangs

"Why don't you fool him sometimes?" I suggested. "Make a nest out of a mustard-plaster and see what he would do."

"He's too old a bird to be caught that way," said Cephalus. "He's a confounded old ass, but he's a brainy one."

At this moment a blare of the most heavenly trumpets sounded, and Cephalus and I left the building and emerged into the garden to see what had caused it. There a dazzling spectacle met my gaze. A regiment of Amazons was drawn up on the green of the parade and a superb gilded coach, drawn by six milk-white horses, stood before them, while two gorgeously apparelled heralds sounded a fanfare. Cephalus immediately became deeply agitated.

"It is his Majesty's own carriage and guard," he cried.

"Whose?" said I.

"Jupiter's," said he. "I fancy they have come for you."

And it so transpired. One of the heralds advanced to where I was standing, saluted me as though I were an emperor, and, through his golden trumpet, informed me that eleven o'clock was approaching; that his Majesty deigned to grant me the desired audience, and had sent a carriage and guard of honor.

I returned the salute, thanked Cephalus for his attentions, and entered the carriage. A brass band of a hundred and twenty pieces struck up an inspiring march, and, preceded and followed by the Amazons, I was conveyed in state to the palatial quarters of Zeus himself.

It suggested comic opera with a large number of pretty chorus girls, but I could not help being impressed in spite of this thought with the fact that Jupiter knew how to do a thing up in style. I was indeed so awed with it all that I did not dare wink at a single Amazon while *en route*, although strongly tempted to do so several times.

IX

SOME ACCOUNT OF THE PALACE OF JUPITER

So dazzled was I by all that went on about me, by the gorgeousness of my equipage and by the extraordinary richness of the costumes worn by my escort, that for the moment I forgot that I was not myself clad in suitable garments for so ultra-royal a function. The streets, the houses, even the throngs that peopled the way, seemed to be of the most lustrous gold, and it became necessary for me from time to time as we progressed to close my eyes and shut out the too brilliant vision. Fancy a bake-shop built of solid gold nuggets, its large plate windows composed each of one huge, flashing diamond; imagine an exquisitely wrought golden drug-store, whose colored jars in the windows are made of rubies, emeralds, and sapphires; conjure up in your mind's eye a sequence of city blocks whose sides are lined by massive and exquisitely proportioned buildings, every inch of whose facade was fashioned, not by stone-cutters and sculptors, but by goldsmiths, whose genius a Cellini might envy; picture to yourself a street paved with golden asphalt, and a sidewalk built from huge slabs of rolled silver, the curb and gutters being of burnished copper, and you'll gain some idea of the thoroughfare along which I passed. And oh, the music that the band gave forth to which the populace timed their huzzas - I nearly went mad with the seductiveness of it all. If it hadn't been for the ache the brilliance of it gave to my eyes, I really think I should have swooned.

John Kendrick Bangs

And then we came to the palace grounds. These, I must confess, I found far from pleasing, for even as the avenue along which I had passed was all gold and silver and gems, so too was the park, in the heart of which stood Jupiter's own apartments made of similar stuff. The trees were golden, and the leaves rustling in the breeze, catching and reflecting the light of the sun, were blinding. The soft greenness of the earthly grass was superseded by the glistening yellow of golden spears, and here and there, where a drop of dew would have fallen, were diamonds of purest ray. The paths were of silken rugs of richest texture, and the palace, as it burst upon my vision, fashioned out of undreamed-of blocks of onyx, resembled more a massive opal filled with flashing, living, fire, than the mere home of a splendid royalty.

I was glad when the procession stopped before the gorgeous entrance to the palace. Another minute of such splendor would have blinded me. A fanfare of trumpets sounded, and I descended, so dizzy with what I had seen that, as my feet touched the ground, I staggered like a drunken man, and then I heard my name sounded and passed from one flunky to another up the magnificent staircase into the blue haze of the hallway, and gradually sounding fainter and fainter until it was lost in the distance of the mysterious corridor. I still staggered as I mounted the steps, and the Major Domo approached me.

"I trust you are not ill," he whispered in my ear.

"No - not ill," I replied. "Only somewhat flabbergasted by all this magnificence, and my eyes hurt like the very deuce."

"It is perhaps too much for mortal eyes," he said; and then, turning to a gilded Ethiopian who stood close at hand, he observed, quietly, "Rhadamus, run over to the Argus and ask him if he can spare this gentleman a pair of blue goggles for an hour or two."

"Better get me a dozen pairs," I put in. "I don't think one pair will be enough. It may strain my nose to hold them, but I'd rather sacrifice my nose than my eyes any day."

But the boy was off, and ere I reached the presence of Jupiter I was very kindly provided with the very essential article, and I must confess that I found great relief in them. They were so densely blue that an ordinary bit of splendor could not have been discerned through their opaque depths, any more than Thisbe could have been seen by her doting lover, Pyramus, through the wall that separated them, but nothing known to man could have shut out the supreme gloriousness of the interior of Jupiter's palace. Even with the goggles of the Argus regulated to protect one thousand eyes upon my nose, it made my dazzled optics blink.

I do not know what the proportions of the palace were. I regret to say that I forgot to ask, but I am quite confident that I walked at least eight miles along that corridor, and never was a mansion designed that was better equipped in the matter of luxuries. I suspect I shall be charged with exaggerating, but it is none the less true that within that spacious building were appliances of every sort known to man. One door opened upon an in-door golf-links, upon which the royal family played whenever they lacked the energy or the disposition to seek out that on Mars. There were high bunkers, the copse of which was covered with richest silk plush, stuffed, I was told, with spun silk, while, in place of sand, tons of powdered sugar and grated nutmegs filled the bunkers themselves. The eighteen holes were laid out so that no two of them crossed, and, inasmuch as the turf was constructed of rubber instead of grass and soil, neither a bad lie nor a dead ball was possible through the vast extent of the fair green. The water hazards, four in number, were nothing more nor less than huge tanks of Burgundy, champagne, iced tea, and Scotch - which I subsequently learned often resulted in a bad caddie service - and an open brook along whose dashing descent a constant stream of shandygaff went merrily bubbling onward to an in-door sea upon which Jupiter exercised his yacht when sailing was the thing to suit his immediate whim.

John Kendrick Bangs

This sea was a marvel. Since all the water hazards above described emptied into it, it was little more than a huge expanse of punch, one swallow of which, thanks to these ingredients and the sugar and nutmeg from the bunkers, would make a man forget an eternity of troubles until he woke up again, if he ever did. Here Jupiter sported every variety of pleasure craft, and, by an ingenious system of funnels arranged about its sixty-square-mile area, could at a moment's notice produce any variety of breeze he chanced to wish; and its submarine bottom was so designed that if a heavy sea were wanted to make the yacht pitch and toss, a simple mechanical device would cause it to hump itself into such corrugations, large or small, as were needed to bring about the desired conditions.

"Do they allow bathing in that?" I asked, as the Major Domo explained the peculiar feature of this in-door sea to me.

My companion laughed. "Only one person ever tried it with any degree of success, and it nearly cost him his reputation. Old Bacchus undertook to swim on a wager from Chambertin Inlet to Glenlivet Bay, but he had to give up before he got as far as Pommery Point. It took him a year to get rid of his headache, and it actually required three-quarters of the Treasury Reserve to provide gold enough to cure him."

"It must be a terrible place to fall overboard in," I suggested.

"It is, if you fall head first," said the Major Domo, "and my observation is that most people do."

"I should admire to sail upon it," I said, gazing back through the door that opened upon Jupiter's yachting parlors, and realizing on a sudden a powerful sense of thirst.

"I have no doubt you can do so," said the Major Domo. "Indeed, I understand that his Majesty contemplates taking you for a sail to the lost island of Atlantis before you return to earth."

"What?" I cried. "The lost island of Atlantis here?"

"Of course," said my guide. "Why not? It was too beautiful for earth, so Jupiter had it transported to his own private yachting pond, and it has been here ever since. It is marvellously beautiful."

Hardly had I recovered from my amazement over the Major Domo's announcement when he pointed to another open door.

"The Royal Arena," he said, simply. "That is where we have our Olympian Games. There was a football game there yesterday. Too bad you were not there. It was the liveliest game of the season. All Hades played the Olympian eleven for the championship of the universe. We licked 'em four hundred to nothing; but of course we had an exceptional team. When Hercules is in shape there isn't a man-jack in all Hades that can withstand him. He's rush-line, centre, full-back, half-back, and flying wedge, all rolled into one. Then the Hades chaps made the bad mistake of sending a star team. When you have an eleven made up of Hannibal and Julius Caesar and Alexander the Great and Napoleon Bonaparte and the Duke of Wellington and Achilles and other fellows like that you can't expect any team-play. Each man is thinking about himself all the time. Hercules could walk right through 'em, and, when they begin to pose, it's mere child's play for him. The only chap that put up any game against us at all was Samson, and I tell you, now that his hair's grown again, he's a demon on the gridiron. But we divided up our force to meet that difficulty. Hercules put the rest of our eleven on to Samson, while he took care, personally, of all the other Hadesians. And you should have seen how he handled them! It was beautiful, all through. He nearly got himself ruled off in the second half. He became so excited at one time towards the end that he mistook Pompey for the ball and kicked him through the goal-posts from the forty-yard line. Of course, it didn't count, and Hercules apologized so gracefully to the rest of the visitors that they withdrew their protest and let him play on."

"I should think he would have apologized to Pompey," said I.

"He will when Pompey recovers consciousness," said my guide, simply.

So interested was I in the Royal Arena and its recent game that I forgot all about Jupiter.

"I never thought of Hercules as a football player before," I said, "but it is easy to see how he might become the champion of Olympus."

"Oh, is it!" laughed the Major Domo. "Well, you'd better not tell Jupiter that. Jupiter'd be pleased, he would. Why, my dear friend, he'd pack you back to earth quicker than a wink. He brooks only one champion of anything here, and that's himself. Hercules threw him in a wrestling-match once, and the next day Jupiter turned him into a weeping-willow, and didn't let up on him for five hundred years afterwards."

By this time we had reached one of the most superbly vaulted chambers it has ever been my pleasure to look upon. Above me the ceiling seemed to reach into infinity, and on either side were huge recesses and alcoves of almost unfathomable depth, lit by great balls of fire that diffused their light softly and yet brilliantly through all parts and corners of the apartment.

"The library," said the Major Domo, pointing to tier upon tier of teeming shelves, upon which stood a wonderful array of exquisitely bound volumes to a number past all counting.

I was speechless with the grandeur of it all.

"It is sublime," said I. "How many volumes?"

"Unnumbered, and unnumberable by mortals, but in round, immortal figures just one jovillion."

"One jovillion, eh?" said I. "How many is that in mortal figures?"

"A jovillion is the supreme number," explained the guide. "It is the infinity of millions, and therefore cannot be expressed in mortal terms."

"Then," said I, "you can have no more books."

"No," said he. "But what of that? We have all there are and all that are to be. You see, the library is divided into three parts. On the right-hand side are all the books that ever have been written; here to the left you see all the books that are being written; and farther along, beginning where that staircase rises, are all the books that ever will be written."

I gasped. If this were true, this wonderful collection must contain my own complete works, some of which I have doubtless not even thought of as yet. How easy it would be for me, I thought, to write my future books if Jupiter would only let me loose here with a competent stenographer to copy off the pages of manuscript as yet undreamed of! I suggested this to the Major Domo.

"He wouldn't let you," he said. "It would throw the whole scheme out of gear."

"I don't see why," I ventured.

"It is simple," rejoined the Major Domo. "If you were permitted to read the books that some day will be identified with your name, as a sensible man, observing beforehand how futile and trivial they are to be, some of them, you wouldn't write them, and so you would be able to avoid a part, at least, of your destiny. If mortals were able to do that - well, they'd become immortals, a good many of them."

I realized the justice of this precaution, and we passed on in silence.

"Now," said the Major Domo, after we had traversed the length of the library, "we are almost there. That gorgeous door directly ahead of you is the entrance to Jupiter's reception-room. Before we enter, however, we must step into the office of Midas, on the left."

"Midas?" I said. "And what, pray, is his function? Is he the registrar?"

"No, indeed," laughed the Major Domo. "I presume down where you live he would be called the Court Tailor. The sartorial requirements of Jupiter are so regal that none of his guests, invited or otherwise, could afford, even with the riches of Cr[oe]sus, to purchase the apparel which he demands. Hence he keeps Midas here to supply, at his expense, the garments in which his visitors may appear before him. You didn't think you were going into Jupiter's presence in those golf duds, did you?"

"I never thought anything about it," said I. "But how long will it take Midas to fit me out?"

"He touches your garments, that's all," said my guide, "and in that instant they are changed to robes of richest gold. We then place a necklace of gems about your neck, composed of rubies, emeralds, amethysts, and sapphires, alternating with pearls, none smaller than a hen's egg; next we place a jewelled staff of ebony in your hand; a golden helmet, having at either side the burnished wings of the imperial eagles of Jove, and bearing upon its crest an opal that glistens like the sun through the slight haze of a translucent cloud, will be placed upon your head; richly decorated sandals of cloth of gold will adorn your feet, and about your waist a girdle of linked diamonds - beside which the far-famed Orloff diamond of the Russian treasury is an insignificant bit of glass - will be clasped."

"And - wha - wha - what becomes of all this when I get back home?" I gasped, a vision of future ease rising before my tired eyes.

"You take it with you, if you can," laughed the Major Domo, with a sly wink at one of the Amazons who accompanied him as a sort of aide.

It was all as he said. In two minutes I had entered the room of Midas; in three minutes, my golf-coat having been removed, a flowing gown of silk, touched by his magic hand and turned to glittering gold, rested upon my shoulders. It was pretty heavy, but I bore up under it; the helmet and the necklace, the shoes and the girdle were adjusted; the staff was placed in my hand, and with beating heart I emerged once more into the corridor and stood before the door leading into the audience-chamber.

"Remove the goggles," whispered the Major Domo.

"Never!" I cried. "I shall be blinded."

"Nonsense!" said he, quickly. "Off with them," and he flicked them from my nose himself.

A great blare of trumpets sounded, the door was thrown wide, and with a cry of amazement I stepped backward, awed and afraid; but one glance was reassuring, for truly a wonderful sight confronted me, and one that will prove as surprising to him who reads as it was to me upon that marvellous day.

X

AN EXTRAORDINARY INTERVIEW

I had expected to witness a scene of grandeur, and my fancy had conjured up, as the central figure thereof, the majestic form of Jove himself, clad in imperial splendor. But it was the unexpected that happened, for, as the door closed behind me, I found myself in a plain sort of workshop, such as an ordinary man would have in his own house, at one end of which stood a rolling-top desk, and, instead of the dazzling throne I had expected to see, there stood in front of it an ordinary office-chair that twirled on a pivot. Books and papers were strewn about the floor and upon the tables; the pictures on the walls were made up largely of colored sporting prints of some rarity, and in a corner stood a commonplace globe such as is to be found in use in public schools to teach children geography. As I glanced about me my first impression was that by some odd mischance I had got into the wrong room, which idea was fortified by the fact that, instead of an imperial figure clad in splendid robes, a quiet-looking old gentleman, who, except for his dress, might have posed for a cartoon of the accepted American Populist, stood before me. He was dressed in a plain frock-coat, four-in-hand tie, high collar, dark-gray trousers, and patent-leather boots, and was brushing up a silk hat as I entered.

"Excuse me, sir," I said, "but I - I fear I have stumbled into the wrong room. I - ah - I have had the wholly unexpected honor to be granted an audience with Jupiter, and I was told that this was the audience-chamber."

"Don't apologize. Sit down," he replied, taking me by the hand and shaking it cordially. "You are all right; I'm glad to see you. How goes the world with you?"

"Very well indeed, sir," I replied, rather embarrassed by the old fellow's cordiality. "But I really can't sit down, because, you know, I - I don't want to keep his Majesty waiting, and if you'll excuse me, I'll -"

"Oh, nonsense!" he retorted. "Let the old man wait. Sit down and talk to me. I don't get a chance to talk with mortals very often. This is your first visit to Olympus?"

"Yes, sir," I said, still standing. "And it is wholly unexpected. I stumbled upon the place by the merest chance last night - but you *must* let me go, sir. I'll come back later very gladly and talk with you if I get a chance. It will never do for me to keep his Majesty waiting, you know."

"Oh, the deuce with his Majesty," said the old gentleman, testily. "What do you want to see him for? He's an old fossil."

"Granted," said I. "Still, I'm interested in old fossils."

The old gentleman roared with laughter at this apparently simple remark. I didn't see the fun of it myself, and his mirth irritated me.

"Excuse me, my dear sir," I said, trying to control my impatience. "But you don't seem to understand my position. I can't stay here and talk to you while the ruler of Olympus waits. Can't you see that?"

"No, I can't," he replied. "Can't see it at all, and I'm a pretty good seer as a general thing, too. If you didn't wish to see me, you had no business to come into my room. Now that you are here, I'm going to keep you for a little while. Take off that absurd-looking tile and sit down."

At this I grew angry. I wasn't responsible for the helmet I wore, and I had felt all along that I looked like an ass in it.

"I'll do nothing of the sort, you confounded old meddler," I cried. "I've come here on invitation, and, if I've got into the wrong room, it isn't my fault. That jackass of a Major Domo told me this was the place. Let me out."

I strode to the doorway, and the old gentleman turned to his desk and opened a drawer.

"Cigar or cigarette?" he said, calmly.

"Neither, you old fool," I retorted, turning the knob and tugging upon it. "I have no time for a smoke."

The door was locked. The old gentleman settled back in his twirling chair and regarded me with a twinkle in his eye as I vainly tried to pull the door open, and I realized that I was helpless.

"Better sit down and enjoy a quiet smoke with me," he said, calmly. "Take off that absurd-looking tile and talk to me."

"I haven't anything to say to you," I replied. "Not a word. Do you intend to let me out of this or not?"

"All in good time - all in good time," he said. "Let's talk it over. Why do you wish to go? Don't you find me good company?"

"You're a stupid old idiot!" I shouted, almost weeping with rage. "Locking me up in your rotten old den here when you must realize what you are depriving me of. What earthly good it does you I can't see."

"It does me lots of good," he said, with a chuckle. "Really, sir, it gives me a new sensation - first new sensation I have had in a long, long time. Let me see now, just how many names have you called me in the three minutes I have had the pleasure of your acquaintance?"

"Give me time, and I'll call you a lot more," I retorted, sullenly.

"Good - I'll give you the time," he said. "Go ahead. I'll listen to you for a whole hour. What am I besides a meddler, and a stupid old idiot, and an old fool?"

"You're a gray-headed maniac, and a - a zinc-fastened Zany. A doddering dotard and a chimerical chump," I said.

"Splendid!" roared he, with a spasm of laughter that seemed nearly to rend him. "Go on. Keep it up. I am enjoying myself hugely."

"You're a sneak-livered poltroon to treat me this way," I added, indignantly.

"That's the best yet," he interrupted, slapping his knee with delight. "Sneak-livered poltroon, eh? Well, well, well. Go on. Go on."

"If you'll give me a copy of Roget's *Thesaurus*, I'll tell you what else you are," I retorted, with a note of sarcasm in my voice. "It will require a reference to that book to do you justice. I can't begin to carry all that you are in my mind."

"With pleasure," said he, and reaching over to his bookcase he took thence the desired volume and handed it to me. "Proceed," he added. "I am all ears."

"Most jackasses are," I returned, savagely.

"Magnificent," he cried, ecstatically. "You are a genius at epithet. But there's the book. Let me light a cigar for you and then you can begin. Only *do* take off that absurd tile. You don't know how supremely unbecoming it is."

There was nothing for it, so I resolved to make the best of it by meeting the disagreeable old pantaloon on his own ground. I lit one of his cigars and sat down to tell the curious old freak what I thought of him. Ordinarily I would have avoided doing this, but his tyrannical exercise of his temporary advantage made me angry to the very core of my being.

"Ready?" said I.

"Quite," said he. "Don't stint yourself. Just behave as if you'd known me all your life. I sha'n't mind."

And I began: "Well, after referring to the word 'idiot' in the index, just to get a lead," I said, "I shall begin by saying that you are evidently a hebetudinous imbecile, an indiscriminate stult -"

"Hold on!" he cried. "What's that last? I never heard the term before."

"Stult - an indiscriminate stult," I said, scornfully. "I invented the word myself. Real words won't describe you. Stult is a new term, meaning all kinds of a fool, plus two. And I've got a few more if you want them."

"Want them?" he cried. "By Vulcan, I dote upon them! They are nectar to my thirsty ears. Go on."

"You are a senseless frivoler, a fugacious gid, an infamous hoddydoddy; you are a man with the hoe with the emptiness of ages in your face; you are a brother to the ox, with all the dundering niziness of a plain, ordinary buzzard added to your shallow-brained asininity. Now will you let me go?"

"Not I," said he, shaking his head as if he relished a situation which was gradually making a madman of me. "I'd like to oblige you, but I really can't. You are giving me too much pleasure. Is there nothing more you can call me?"

"You're a dizzard!" I retorted. "And a noodle and a jolt-head; you're a jobbernowl and a doodle, a maundering mooncalf and a blockheaded numps, a gaby and a loon; you're a *Hatter*!" I shrieked the last epithet.

"Heavens!" he cried, "A Hatter! Am I as bad as that?"

"Oh, come now," I said, closing the *Thesaurus* with a bang. "Have some regard for my position, won't you?"

I had resolved to appeal to his better nature. "I don't know who the dickens you are. You may be the three wise men of Gotham who went to sea in a bowl rolled into one, for all I know. You may be any old thing. I don't give a tinker's cuss what you are. Under ordinary circumstances I've no doubt I should find you a very pleasant old gentleman, but under present conditions you are a blundering old bore."

"That's not bad - indeed, a blundering old bore is pretty good. Let me see," he continued, looking up the word "bore" in the index of the *Thesaurus*, "What else am I? Maybe I'm an unmitigated nuisance, an exasperating and egregious glum, a carking care, and a pestiferous pill, eh?"

"You are all of that," I said, wearily. "Your meanness surpasseth all things. I've met a good many tough characters in my day, but you are the first I have ever encountered without a redeeming feature. You take advantage of a mistake for which I am not at all responsible, and what do you do?"

"Tell me," he replied. "What do I do? I shall be delighted to hear. I've been asking myself that question for years. What do I do? Go on, I implore you."

"You rub it in, that's what," I retorted. "You take advantage of me. You bait me; you incommode me. You - you -"

"Here, take the *Thesaurus*," he said, as I hesitated for the word. "It will help you. I provoke you, I irritate you, I make you mad, I sour your temper, I sicken, disgust, revolt, nauseate, repel you. I rankle your soul. I jar you - is that it?"

"Give me the book," I cried, desperately. "Yes!" I added, referring to the page. "You tease, irk, harry, badger, infest, persecute. You gall, sting, and convulse me. You are a plain old beast, that's what you are. You're a conscienceless sneak and a wherret - you mean-souled blot on the face of nature!"

Here I broke down and wept, and the old gentleman's sides shook with laughter. He was, without exception, the most extraordinary old person I had ever encountered, and in my tears I cursed the English language because it was inadequate properly to describe him.

For a time there was silence. I was exhausted and my tormentor was given over to his own enjoyment of my discomfiture. Finally, however, he spoke.

"I'm a pretty old man, my dear fellow," he said. "I shouldn't like to tell you how old, because if I did you'd begin on the *Thesaurus* again with the word 'liar' for your lead. Nevertheless, I'm pretty old; but I want to say to you that in all my experience I have never had so diverting a half-hour as you have given me. You have been so outspoken, so frank -"

"Oh, indeed - I've been frank, have I?" I interrupted. "Well, what I have said isn't a marker to what I'd like to have said and would have said if language hadn't its limitations. You are the infinity of the unmitigated, the supreme of the superfluous. In unqualified, inexcusable, unsurpassable meanness you are the very IT!"

"Sir," said the old gentleman, rising and bowing, "you are a man of unusual penetration, and I like you. I should like to see more of you, but your hour has expired. I thank you for your pleasant words, and I bid you an affectionate good-morning."

A deep-toned bell struck the hour of twelve. A fanfare of trumpets sounded outside, and the huge door flew open, and without a word in reply, glad of my deliverance, I turned and fled precipitately through it. The sumptuous guard stood outside to receive me, and as the door closed behind me the band struck up a swelling measure that I shall not soon forget.

"Well," said the Major Domo, as we proceeded back to my quarters, "did he receive you nicely?"

"Who?" said I.

"Jupiter, of course," he said.

"I didn't see him," I replied, sadly. "I fell in with a beastly old bore who wouldn't let go of me. You showed me into the wrong room. Who was that old beggar, anyhow?"

"Beggar?" he cried. "Wrong room? Beggar?"

"Certainly," said I. "Beggar is mild, I admit. But he's all that and much more. Who is he?"

"I don't know what you mean," replied the Major Domo. "But you have been for the last hour with his Majesty himself."

"What?" I cried. "I - that old man - we -"

"The old gentleman was Jupiter. Didn't he tell you? He made a special effort to make you feel at home - put himself on a purely mortal basis -"

I fell back, limp and nerveless.

"What will he think of me?" I moaned, as I realized what had happened.

"He thinks you are the best yet," said the Major Domo. "He has sent word by his messenger, Mercury, that the honors of

John Kendrick Bangs

Olympus are to be showered upon you to their fullest extent. He says you are the only frank mortal he ever met."

And with this I was escorted back to my rooms at the hotel, impressed with the idea that all is not lead that doesn't glitter, and when I thought of my invention of the word "stult," I began to wish I had never been born.

XI

A ROYAL OUTING

As may be imagined after my untoward interview with Jupiter, the state of my mind was far from easy. It is not pleasant to realize that you have applied every known epithet of contempt to a god who has an off-hand way of disposing of his enemies by turning them into apple-trees, or dumb beasts of one kind or another, and upon retiring to my room I sat down and waited in great dread of what should happen next. I couldn't really believe that the Major Domo's statement as to my having been forgiven was possible. It predicated too great a magnanimity to be credible.

"I hope to gracious he won't make a pine-tree of me," I groaned, visions of a future in which woodmen armed with axes, and sawmills, played a conspicuous part, rising up before me. "I'd hate like time to be sawed up into planks and turned into a Georgia pine floor somewhere."

It was a painful line of thought and I strove to get away from it, but without success, although the variations were interesting when I thought of all the things I might be made into, such as kitchen tables, imitation oak bookcases, or perhaps - horror of horrors - a bundle of toothpicks! I was growing frantic with fear, when on a sudden my reveries of dread were interrupted by a knock on the door.

"It has come at last!" I said, and I opened the door, nerving myself up to sustain the blow which I believed was impending. Mercury stood without, flapping the wings that sprouted from his ankles impatiently.

"The skitomobile is ready, sir," he said.

I gazed at him earnestly.

"The what?"

"The skitomobile, to take you to the links. Jupiter has already gone on ahead, and he has commanded me to follow, bringing you along with me."

"Oh - I'm to go to the links, eh? What's he going to do with me when he gets me there? Turn me into a golf-ball and drive me off into space?" I inquired.

My heart sank at the very idea, but I was immediately reassured by Mercury's hearty laugh.

"Of course not - why should he? He's going to play you an eighteen-hole match. You've made a great impression on the old gentleman."

"Thank Heaven!" I said. "I'll hurry along and join him before he changes his mind."

In a brief while I was ready, and, escorted by Mercury, I was taken to the skitomobile which stood at the exit from the hall to the outer roadway nearest my room. Seated in front of this, and acting as chauffeur, was a young man whom I recognized at once as Phaeton. Alongside of him sat Jason, polishing up the most beautiful set of golf-clubs I ever saw. The irons were of wrought gold, and the shafts of the most highly polished and exquisite woods.

"To the links," said Mercury, and with a sudden chug-chug, and a jerk which nearly threw me out of the conveyance, we were off. And what a ride it was! At first the sensation was that of falling, and I clutched nervously at the sides of the skitomobile, but by slow degrees I got used to it, and enjoyed one of the most exhilarating hours that has ever entered into my experience.

Planet after planet was passed as we sped on and on upward, and as my delight grew I gave utterance to it.

"Jove! But this is fine!" I said. "I never knew anything like it, except looping the loop."

Phaeton grinned broadly and winked at Jason.

"How would you like to loop the loop out here?" the latter asked.

"What? In a machine like this?" I cried.

"Certainly," said Jason. "It's great sport. Give him the twist, Phaeton."

I began to grow anxious again, for I recalled the past careless methods of Phaeton, and I had no wish to go looping the loop through the empyrean with one of his known adventurous disposition, to be hurled unceremoniously sooner or later perhaps into the sun itself.

"Perhaps we'd better leave it until some other day," I ventured, timidly.

"No time like the present," Jason retorted. "Only hang on to yourself. All ready, Phaety!"

The chauffeur grasped the lever, and, turning it swiftly to one side, there in the blue vault of heaven, a thousand miles from anywhere, that machine began executing the most remarkable flip-flaps the mind of man ever conceived. Not once or twice, but a hundred times did we go whirling round and round through the skies, until finally I got so that I could not tell if I were right side up or upside down. It was great sport, however, and but for the fact that on the third trial I lost my grip and would have fallen head over heels through space had not Mercury, who was flying alongside of the machine, swooped down and caught me by the leg as I fell out, I found it as exhilarating as it was novel. I could have kept it up forever, had we not shortly hove in sight of the links, which, as I have already told you, were located on the planet Mars; and such gorgeousness as I there encountered was unparalleled on earth. Much that we earth-folk have wondered at became clear at once. The great canals, as we call them, for instance, turned out to be vast sand-bunkers that glistened like broad rivers of silver in the wondrous sheen of the planet, while the dark greenish spots, concerning which our astronomers have speculated so variously, were nothing more nor less than putting-greens. It is extraordinary that until my visit to the planet as the guest of Jupiter, this perfectly simple solution of the various Martian problems was not even guessed.

As we drew up at the pretty little club-house, Jupiter emerged from the door and greeted me cordially. My eyes fell before his smiling gaze, for I must confess I was mighty shamefaced over my experience of the morning, but his manner restored my self-possession. It was very genial and forgiving.

"Glad to see you again," he said. "If you play golf as well as you do synonyms you're a scratch man. You didn't foozle a syllable."

"I should have, had I known as much as I do now," said I.

"Well, I'm glad you didn't know," Jupiter returned majestically, "for I can use that word stult in my business. Now suppose we have a bit of luncheon and then start out."

After eating sparingly we began our game. I was provided with a caddie that looked like one of Raphael's angels, and Jupiter himself handed me a driver from his own bag.

"You'll have to be careful how you use it," he said; "it has properties which may astonish you."

I teed up my ball, swung back, and then with all the vigor at my command whacked the ball square and true. It sprang from the tee like a bird let loose and flew beyond my vision, and while I was trying with my eye to keep up with it in its flight, I received a stinging blow on the back of my head which felled me to the ground.

"Thunderation!" I roared. "What was that?"

Jupiter laughed. "It was your own ball," he said. "You put too much muscle into that stroke, and, as a consequence, the ball flew all the way round the planet and clipped you from behind."

"You don't mean to say -" I began.

"Yes, I do," said Jupiter. "That is a special long-distance driver made for me. Only had it two days. It is not easy to use, because it has such wonderful force. Hercules drove a ball three times around the planet at one stroke with it yesterday. To use it properly requires judgment. Up here you have to play golf with your head, as well as with your clubs."

"Well, I played it with mine all right," I put in, rubbing the lump on the back of my head ruefully. "Shall I play two?"

"Certainly," said Jupiter. "You've a good brassey lie behind the tee there. Play gently now, for this hole isn't more than three hundred miles long."

My brassey stroke is one of my best, and I did myself proud. The ball flew about one hundred and seventy-nine miles in a straight line, but landed in a sand-bunker. Jupiter followed with a good clean drive for two hundred miles, breaking all the records previously stated to me by Adonis, whereupon we entered the skitomobile and were promptly transported to the edge of the bunker, where my ball reposed upon the glistening sand. It took three to get out, owing to the height of the cop, which rose a trifle higher in the air than Mount Blanc, but the niblick Jason had brought along for my use, as soon as I got used to the titanic quality of the game I was playing, was finally equal to the loft. My ball landed just short of the green, one hundred and sixteen miles away. Jupiter foozled his approach, and we both reached the edge of the green in four.

"Bully distance for a putt," said Jupiter, taking the line from his ball to the hole.

"About how far is it?" I asked, for I couldn't see anything resembling a hole within a mile of me.

"Oh, five miles, I imagine," was the answer. "Put on these glasses and you'll see the disk."

My courteous host handed me a pair of spectacles which I put upon my nose, and there, seemingly two inches away, but in reality five and a quarter miles, was the hole. The glasses were a revelation, but I had seen too much that was wonderful to express surprise.

"Dead easy," I said, referring to the putt, now that I had the glasses on.

"Looks so," said Jupiter, "but be careful. You can't hope to putt until you know your ball."

At the moment I did not understand, but a minute after I had a shock. Putting perfectly straight, the ball rolled easily along and then made a slight hitch backward, as if I had put a cut on it, and struck off ahead, straight as an arrow but to the left of the disk. This it continued to do in its course, zigzagging more and more out of the straight line until it finally stopped, quite two and a half miles from the cup.

"Now watch me," said Jupiter. "You'll get an idea of how the ball works."

I obeyed, and was surprised to see him aim at a point at least a mile aside of the mark, but the results were perfect, for the gutty, acting precisely as mine did, zigzagged along until it reached the rim of the cup and then dropped gently in.

"One up," said Jupiter, with a broad smile as he watched my ill-repressed wonderment.

As we were transported to the next tee by Phaeton and his machine, I looked at my ball, and the peculiarity of its make became clear at once. It was called "The Vulcan," and in action had precisely the same movement as that of a thunder-bolt - thus:

"Great ball, eh?" said Jupiter. "Adds a lot to the science of the game. A straight putt is easy, but the zigzag is no child's play."

"I think I shall like it," I said, "if I ever get used to it."

The second hole reached, I was astonished to see a huge apparatus like a cannon on the tee, and in fact that is what it turned out to be.

"We call this the Cannon Hole," said Jupiter. "It lends variety to the game. It's a splendid test of your accuracy, and if you don't make it in one you lose it. If you will put on those glasses you will see the hole, which is in the middle of a target. You've got to go through it at one stroke."

"That isn't golf, is it?" I asked. "It's marksmanship."

"I call it so," said Jupiter, calmly. "And what I say goes. Moreover, it requires much skill to offset the effect of the wind."

"But there is none," said I.

"There will be," said Jupiter, putting his ball in the cannon's breach and making ready to drive. "You see those huge steel affairs on either side of the course, that look like the ventilators on an ocean steamer?"

"Yes," said I, for as I looked I perceived that this part of the course was studded with them.

"Well, they supply the wind," said Jupiter. "I just ring a bell and AEolus sets his bellows going, and I tell you the winds you get are cyclonic, and, best of all, they blow in all directions. From the first ventilator the wind is northeast by south; from the second it is southwest by north-northeast; from the third it is straight north, and so on. Winds are blowing at the moment of play from all possible points of the compass. Fore!"

A bell rang, and never in a wide experience in noises had I ever before heard such a fearful din as followed. A hurricane sprang from one point, a gale from another, a cyclone from a third - such an aeolian purgatory was never let loose in my sight before, but Jupiter, gauging each and all, fired his ball from the cannon, and it sped on, buffeted here and there, now up, now down, like a bit of fluff in the chance zephyrs of the spring-tide, but ultimately passing through the hole in the target, and landing gently in a basket immediately behind the bull's-eye. The winds immediately died down, and all was quiet again.

"Perfectly great!" I said, with enthusiasm, for it did seem marvellous. "But I don't think I can do it. You win, of course."

"Not at all," said Jupiter. "If you hit the bull's-eye, as I did, you win."

"And you lose in spite of that splendid - er - stroke?" I asked.

"Oh no - not at all," said Jupiter. "We both win."

Again the bell rang, and the winds blew, and the cannon shot, but my ball, under the excitement of the moment of aiming, was directed not towards the bull's-eye - or the hole - but at the skitomobile. It hit it fairly and hard, and it smashed the engine by which the machine was propelled, much to the consternation of Jason and Phaeton.

"Unfortunate," said Jupiter. "Very. But never mind. We don't have to walk home."

"I'm awfully sorry," said I. "I - er -"

"Never mind," said Jupiter. "It is easily repaired, but we cannot go on with the game. The next hole is eight thousand miles long. Twice around the planet, and we couldn't possibly walk it, so we'll have to quit. We've got all we can manage trudging back to the club-house. Here, caddies, take our clubs back to the club-house, and tell 'em to have two nectar highballs ready at six-thirty. Phaeton, you and Jason will have to get back the best way you can. I've told you a half-dozen times to bring two machines with you, but you never seem to understand. Come along, Higgins, we'll go back. Shut your eyes."

I closed my optics, as ordered, although my name is not Higgins, and I didn't like to have even Jupiter so dub me.

"Now open them again," was the sharp order.

I did so, and lo and behold! by some supernatural power we had been transported back to the club-house.

"I am sorry, Jupiter," said I "to have spoiled your game," as we sat, later, sipping that delicious concoction, the nectar highball, which we supplemented with a "Pegasus's neck."

"Nonsense," said he, grandly. "You haven't spoiled my *game*. You have merely, without meaning to do so, spoiled your own afternoon. My game is all right and will remain so. It would have been a great pleasure to me to show you the other sixteen holes, but circumstances were against us. Take your nectar and let us trot along. You dine with Juno and myself to-night. Let's see, I was two up, wasn't I?"

"Two up, and sixteen to play."

"Then I win," said he. It was an extraordinary score, but then it was an extraordinary occasion.

And we entered his chariot, and were whirled back to Olympus. The ride home was not as exciting as the ride out, but it was interesting. It lasted about a half of a millionth of a second, and for the first time in my life I knew how a telegram feels when it travels from New York to San Francisco, and gets there apparently three hours before it is sent by the clock.

XII

I AM DISMISSED

It was a very interesting programme for my further
entertainment that Jupiter mapped out on our way back from
the links, and I deeply regret that an untoward incident that
followed later, for which I was unintentionally responsible,
prevented its being carried out. I was to have been taken off on
a cruise on the inland sea, to where the lost island of Atlantis
was to be found; a special tournament at ping-pong was to be
held in my honor, in which minor planets were to be used
instead of balls, and the players were to be drawn from among
the Titans, who were retained to perform feats of valor, skill,
and strength for Jupiter. The forge of Vulcan was to be visited,
and many of the mysteries of the centre of the earth were to be
revealed, and, best of all, Jupiter himself had promised to give
me an exhibition of his own skill as a marksman in the hurling
of thunder-bolts, and *I was to select the objects to be hit!* Think
of it! What a chance lay here for a man to be rid of certain
things on earth that he did not like! What a vast amount of
ugly American architecture one could be rid of in the
twinkling of an eye! What a lot of enemies and eyesores it was
now in my power to have removed by an electrical process
availed of in the guise of sport! I spent an hour on that list of
targets, and if only I had been allowed to prolong my stay in
the home of the gods, the world itself would have benefited,
for I was not altogether personal in my selection of things for
Jupiter to aim at. There was Tammany Hall, for instance, and
the Boxers of China - these led my list. There were four or five

John Kendrick Bangs

sunlight-destroying, sky-scraping office buildings in New York and elsewhere; nuisances of every kind that I could think of were put down - the headquarters of the Beef Trust and a few of its sponsors; the editorial offices of the peevish and bilious newspapers, which deny principles and right motives to all save themselves; a regiment of alleged humorists who make jokes about the mother-in-law and other sacred relations of life; an opera-box full of the people who hum every number of Wagner and Verdi through, and keep other people from hearing the singers; row after row of theatre-goers who come in late and trample over the virtuous folk who have arrived punctually; any number of theatrical managers who mistake gloom for amusement; three or four smirking matinee idols, whose talents are measured by the fit of their clothes, the length of their hair, and their ability to spit supernumeraries with a tin sword; cab-drivers who had overcharged me; insolent railway officials; the New York Central Tunnel - indeed, the completed list stretches on to such proportions that it would require more pages than this book contains to present them in detail. I even thought of including Hippopopolis in the list, but when I realized that it was entirely owing to his villany that I had enjoyed the delightful privilege of visiting the gods in their own abode, I spared him. And to think that because of an unintentional error this great opportunity to rid the world, and incidentally myself, of much that is vexatious was wholly lost is a matter of sincere grief to myself.

It happened in this way: Hardly had I returned to my delightful apartment at the hotel, when a messenger arrived bearing a superbly engraved command from Jupiter to dine with himself and Juno *en famille*. It was a kind, courteous, and friendly note, utterly devoid of formality, and we were to spend the evening at cards. Jupiter had indicated in the afternoon that he would like to learn bridge, and, inasmuch as I never travel anywhere without a text-book upon that fascinating subject, I had volunteered to teach him. The dinner was given largely to enable me to do this, and, moreover, Jupiter was quite anxious to have me meet his family, and promised me that before the evening was over I should hear some music from the lyre of Apollo, meet all the muses, and enjoy a chafing-dish snack prepared by the fair hand of Juno herself.

"I'll have Polyphemus up to give us a few coon songs if you like them," he added, "and altogether I can promise you a delightful evening. We drop all our state at these affairs, and I know you'll enjoy yourself."

"I shall feel a trifle embarrassed in the presence of so many gods and goddesses, I am afraid," I put in.

"I'll fix you out as to that," Jupiter replied. "I'll change you for the time being into a god yourself, if you wish."

I laughed at the idea.

"A high old god I'd make," said I.

"You'd pass," he observed, quietly. "I'll call you Pencillius, god of Chirography - or would you rather come as Nonsensius, the newly discovered deity of Jocosity?"

"I think I'd rather be Zero, god of Nit," said I, and it was so ordained.

Of course, I accepted the invitation and was on hand at the palace, as I thought, promptly. As a matter of fact, my watch having in some mysterious fashion been affected by the excitement of the adventure, got galloping away just as my own heart had done more than once. The result was that, instead of arriving at the palace at eight o'clock, as I was expected to do, I got there at seven. Of course, my exalted hosts were not ready to receive me, and there were no other guests to bear me company and keep me out of mischief in the drawing-room, where for an hour I was compelled to wait. At first all went well. I found much entertainment in the room, and on the centre-table, a beautiful bit of furniture, carved out of one huge amethyst, I discovered a number of books and magazines, which kept me tolerably busy for a half-hour. There was a finely bound copy of *Don'ts for the Gods, or Celestial Etiquette*, in which I found many valuable hints on the procedure of Olympian society - notably one injunction as to the use of finger-bowls, from which I learned that the gods in their lavishness have a bowl for each finger; and a little volume by Bacchus on *Intemperance*, which I wish I might publish for the benefit of my fellow-mortals. All I remember about it at the moment of writing is that the author seriously enjoins upon his readers the wickedness of drinking more than sixty cocktails a day, and utterly deprecates the habit of certain Englishmen of drinking seven bottles of port at a sitting. Bacchus seemed to think that, with the other wines incidental to a dinner, no one, not even an Englishman, should attempt to absorb more than five bottles of port over his coffee. It struck me as being rather good advice.

Wearying of the reading at the end of a half-hour, I began a closer inspection of the room and its contents. It was full of novelties, and, naturally, gorgeous past all description; but what most excited my curiosity was a small cabinet, not unlike a stereoscope in shape, which stood in one corner of the room. It had a button at one side, over which was a gilt tablet marked "Push." On its front was the legend, "Drop a Nickel in the Slot, Push the Button, and See the Future." I followed the instructions eagerly. The nickel was dropped, the button pushed, and, putting my eyes before the lenses, I gazed into the remotest days to come. I had come across the Futuroscope, otherwise a kinetoscope with the gift of prophecy. The coming year passed rapidly, and I saw what fate had in store for the world for the twelve months immediately ahead of me; then followed a decade, then a century, and then others, until, just as I was approaching the dread cataclysm which is to mark the end of all mortal things, I heard a quick, startled voice back of me.

It was that of Jupiter, and his tone was a strange mixture of wrath and regret.

"What on earth have you done?" he cried.

"Nothing, your Majesty," said I, shaking all over as with the ague at the revelations I had just witnessed, "except getting a bird's-eye view of what is to come."

"I am sorry," said he, gravely. "It is not well that mortals should know the future, and your imprudent act is destructive of all the plans I have had for you. You must leave us instantly, for that instrument is for the gods alone. Moreover, the knowledge of that which you have seen -"

Here his voice positively thundered, and the frown that came upon his brow filled me with awe and terror.

"All knowledge of what you have seen must be removed from your brain," he added, grimly.

I was speechless with fear as the ruler of Olympus touched an electric button at the side of the room, and the two huge slaves, Gog and Magog, appeared.

"Seize him!" Jupiter commanded, sternly.

In an instant I was bound hand and foot.

"To the office of Dr. AEsculapius!" he commanded, and I was unceremoniously removed to the room wherein I had had my interview with the great doctor, where I was immediately etherized and my brain operated upon. Precisely what was done to me I shall probably never know, but what I do know is that from that time to this all that I saw in that marvellous Futuroscope is a blank, although on all other subjects pertaining to my visit to the gods my recollection is perfectly clear. It suffices to say that I lay for a long time in a stupor, and when finally I came to my senses again I found myself comfortably ensconced in my own bed, in my own home; not in Greece, but in America; suffering from a dull headache from which I did not escape for at least three hours. Again and again and again have I tried to recall that wonderful picture of a marvellous future seen by my mortal eyes that night upon Olympus, that I might set it upon paper for others to read, but with each effort the dreadful pain in the top of my head returns and I find myself compelled to abandon the project.

So was my brief visit to Olympus begun and ended. In its results it has perhaps been neither elevating nor remarkably instructive, but it has given me a better understanding of, and a better liking for, that great company of mythological beings who used to preside over the destinies of the Greeks. They appeared more human than godlike to my eyes. They were companionable to a degree, and for a time, at least, would prove congenial associates for a summer outing, but as a steady diet - well, I am not at all surprised that, as men waxed more mature in years and in experience, these titanic members of the Olympian four hundred lost their power and became no greater factor in the life of the large society of mankind than any other group of people, equal in number and of seeming importance, whose days and nights are given over solely to pleasure and the morbid pursuit of notoriety.

Choose from Thousands of 1stWorldLibrary Classics By

Ada Leverson	Charles Ives	Evelyn Everett-green
Adolphus William Ward	Charles Kingsley	Everard Cotes
Aesop	Charles Klein	F. H. Cheley
Agatha Christie	Charles Lathrop Pack	F. J. Cross
Alexander Aaronsohn	Charles Whibley	Federick Austin Ogg
Alexander Kielland	Charles Willing Beale	Ferdinand Ossendowski
Alexandre Dumas	Charlotte M. Braeme	Francis Bacon
Alfred Gatty	Charlotte M. Yonge	Francis Darwin
Alfred Ollivant	Charlotte Perkins Stetson	Frances Hodgson Burnett
Alice Duer Miller	Clair W. Hayes	Frances Parkinson Keyes
Alice Turner Curtis	Clarence Day Jr.	Frank Gee Patchin
Alice Dunbar	Clarence E. Mulford	Frank Harris
Ambrose Bierce	Clemence Housman	Frank Jewett Mather
Amelia E. Barr	Confucius	Frank L. Packard
Andrew Lang	Cornelis DeWitt Wilcox	Frank V. Webster
Andrew McFarland Davis	Cyril Burleigh	Frederic Stewart Isham
Andy Adams	D. H. Lawrence	Frederick Trevor Hill
Anna Sewell	Daniel Defoe	Frederick Winslow Taylor
Annie Besant	David Garnett	Friedrich Kerst
Annie Hamilton Donnell	Don Carlos Janes	Friedrich Nietzsche
Annie Payson Call	Donald Keyhoe	Fyodor Dostoyevsky
Annonaymous	Dorothy Kilner	G.A. Henty
Anton Chekhov	Dougan Clark	G.K. Chesterton
Arnold Bennett	Douglas Fairbanks	Gabrielle E. Jackson
Arthur Conan Doyle	E. Nesbit	Garrett P. Serviss
Arthur M. Winfield	E.P.Roe	Gaston Leroux
Arthur Ransome	E. Phillips Oppenheim	George Ade
Atticus	Edgar Rice Burroughs	Geroge Bernard Shaw
B.H. Baden-Powell	Edith Van Dyne	George Durston
B. M. Bower	Edith Wharton	George Ebers
Baroness Emmuska Orczy	Edward J. O'Biren	George Eliot
Baroness Orczy	Edward S. Ellis	George MacDonald
Basil King	Edwin L. Arnold	George Meredith
Bayard Taylor	Eleanor Atkins	George Orwell
Ben Macomber	Eliot Gregory	George Tucker
Bertha Muzzy Bower	Elizabeth Gaskell	George W. Cable
Bjornstjerne Bjornson	Elizabeth McCracken	George Wharton James
Booth Tarkington	Elizabeth Von Arnim	Gertrude Atherton
Boyd Cable	Ellem Key	Grace E. King
Bram Stoker	Emerson Hough	Grace Gallatin
C. Collodi	Emily Dickinson	Grant Allen
C. E. Orr	Enid Bagnold	Guillermo A. Sherwell
C. M. Ingleby	Enilor Macartney Lane	Gulielma Zollinger
Carolyn Wells	Erasmus W. Jones	Gustav Flaubert
Catherine Parr Traill	Ernie Howard Pie	H. A. Cody
Charles A. Eastman	Ethel Turner	H. B. Irving
Charles Dickens	Ethel Watts Mumford	H.C. Bailey
Charles Dudley Warner	Eugenie Foa	H. G. Wells
Charles Farrar Browne	Eugene Wood	H. H. Munro

H. Irving Hancock
H. Rider Haggard
H. W. C. Davis
Hamilton Wright Mabie
Hans Christian Andersen
Harold Avery
Harold McGrath
Harriet Beecher Stowe
Harry Houidini
Helent Hunt Jackson
Helen Nicolay
Hendrik Conscience
Hendy David Thoreau
Henri Barbusse
Henrik Ibsen
Henry Adams
Henry Ford
Henry Frost
Henry James
Henry Jones Ford
Henry Seton Merriman
Henry W Longfellow
Herbert A. Giles
Herbert N. Casson
Herman Hesse
Homer
Honore De Balzac
Horace Walpole
Horatio Alger Jr.
Howard Pyle
Howard R. Garis
Hugh Lofting
Hugh Walpole
Humphry Ward
Ian Maclaren
Inez Haynes Gillmore
Irving Bacheller
Israel Abrahams
Ivan Turgenev
J.G.Austin
J. Henri Fabre
J. M. Barrie
J. Macdonald Oxley
J. S. Fletcher
J. S. Knowles
J. Storer Clouston
Jack London
Jacob Abbott
James Allen
James Andrews
James Baldwin

James DeMille
James Joyce
James Lane Allen
James Lane Allen
James Oliver Curwood
James Oppenheim
James Otis
James R. Driscoll
Jane Austen
Jens Peter Jacobsen
Jerome K. Jerome
John Burroughs
John Cournos
John F. Kennedy
John Gay
John Glasworthy
John Habberton
John Joy Bell
John Kendrick Bangs
John Milton
John Philip Sousa
Jonas Lauritz Idemil Lie
Jonathan Swift
Joseph A. Altsheler
Joseph Carey
Joseph Conrad
Joseph E. Badger Jr
Joseph Hergesheimer
Joseph Jacobs
Julian Hawthrone
Julies Vernes
Justin Huntly McCarthy
Kakuzo Okakura
Kenneth Grahame
Kenneth McGaffey
Kate Langley Bosher
Kate Langley Bosher
Katherine Cecil Thurston
Katherine Stokes
L. A. Abbot
L. T. Meade
L. Frank Baum
Latta Griswold
Laura Lee Hope
Laurence Housman
Leo Tolstoy
Leonid Andreyev
Lewis Carroll
Lilian Bell
Lloyd Osbourne
Louis Tracy

Louisa May Alcott
Lucy Fitch Perkins
Lucy Maud Montgomery
Lydia Miller Middleton
Lyndon Orr
M. Corvus
M. H. Adams
Margaret E. Sangster
Margaret Vandercook
Margret Penrose
Maria Edgeworth
Maria Thompson Daviess
Mariano Azuela
Marion Polk Angellotti
Mark Overton
Mark Twain
Mary Austin
Mary Catherine Crowley
Mary Cole
Mary Hastings Bradley
Mary Roberts Rinehart
Mary Rowlandson
M. Wollstonecraft Shelley
Maud Lindsay
Max Beerbohm
Myra Kelly
Nathaniel Hawthrone
Nicolo Machiavelli
O. F. Walton
Oscar Wilde
Owen Johnson
P.G. Wodehouse
Paul and Mabel Thorne
Paul G. Tomlinson
Paul Severing
Percy Brebner
Peter B. Kyne
Plato
R. Derby Holmes
R. L. Stevenson
R. S. Ball
Rabindranath Tagore
Rahul Alvares
Ralph Henry Barbour
Ralph Waldo Emmerson
Rene Descartes
Rex Beach
Rex E. Beach
Richard Harding Davis
Richard Jefferies
Richard Le Gallienne

Robert Barr	Swami Parmananda	Wilkie Collins
Robert Frost	T. S. Ackland	Willa Cather
Robert Gordon Anderson	T. S. Arthur	Willard F. Baker
Robert L. Drake	The Princess Der Ling	William Dean Howells
Robert Lansing	Thomas A. Janvier	William le Queux
Robert Lynd	Thomas A Kempis	W. Makepeace Thackeray
Robert Michael Ballantyne	Thomas Anderton	William W. Walter
Robert W. Chambers	Thomas Bailey Aldrich	Winston Churchill
Rosa Nouchette Carey	Thomas Bulfinch	Yei Theodora Ozaki
Rudyard Kipling	Thomas De Quincey	Yogi Ramacharaka
Samuel B. Allison	Thomas H. Huxley	Young E. Allison
Samuel Hopkins Adams	Thomas Hardy	Zane Grey
Sarah Bernhardt	Thomas More	
Selma Lagerlof	Thornton W. Burgess	
Sherwood Anderson	U. S. Grant	
Sigmund Freud	Valentine Williams	
Standish O'Grady	Various Authors	
Stanley Weyman	Victor Appleton	
Stella Benson	Virginia Woolf	
Stephen Crane	Walter Camp	
Stewart Edward White	Walter Scott	
Stijn Streuvels	Washington Irving	
Swami Abhedananda	Wilbur Lawton